TWO CAKES
FIT FOR A KING

Two Cakes
Fit for a King

Folktales from Vietnam

ꕥꕥꕥꕥꕥꕥꕥꕥꕥꕥꕥꕥꕥꕥꕥꕥꕥ

Compiled by

Nguyen Nguyet Cam and Dana Sachs

Introduced and Illustrated by

Bui Hoai Mai

A Latitude 20 Book
University of Hawai'i Press
Honolulu

© 2003 University of Hawai`i Press

Printed in the United States of America

08 07 06 05 04 03   6 5 4 3 2 1

Library of Congress Cataloging-in-Publication Data
Nguyên, Nguyêt Câm.
  Two cakes fit for a king : folktales from Vietnam / compiled by Nguyen
Nguyet Cam and Dana Sachs ; illustrated by Bui Hoai Mai.
    p.   cm.
  "A latitude 20 book."
  Includes bibliographical references.
  ISBN 0-8248-2668-X (alk. paper)
  1. Tales—Vietnam.   I. Sachs, Dana.   II. Title

GR313.N34 2003
398.2'09597'02—dc21
                                        2003048400

University of Hawai`i Press books are printed on acid-free
paper and meet the guidelines for permanence and
durability of the Council on Library Resources.

Designed by Trina Stahl

Printed by Versa Press, Inc.

For our children:
Alexander Thien and Isaac Thi Zinoman,
Jesse Emile and Samuel Avram Berliner-Sachs,
and Bui Hoai Nam Son and Bui Hoai Nam Minh.

CONTENTS

ACKNOWLEDGMENTS

WE VERY MUCH appreciate the thoughtful comments on the manuscript that we received from Peter Zinoman, Todd Berliner, Nguyen Vo Thu Huong, Le Thi Tham Van, Robert Byington, Philip Gerard, and Sherry Goodman. We thank James Borton, Nguyen Da Huong, and our editor, Masako Ikeda, for their steadfast support of our book, and we are grateful to Nguyen An Thi for his role in inspiring James to become involved in this project. We thank our parents Le Thi Kim Chi and Nguyen Cong Minh, Diane Sachs and Ira Sachs, and Nguyen Thi Mong Bich for nurturing our love for stories. And, for their love and support, we thank our families.

—Nguyen Nguyet Cam, Dana Sachs, and Bui Hoai Mai

Two Cakes
Fit for a King

INTRODUCTION

BY

Bui Hoai Mai

TRANSLATED BY

Nguyen Nguyet Cam and Dana Sachs

A POOR BOY becomes king. A beautiful princess marries the most worthy suitor. The gods play capricious games with the lives of mortals. Such stories and themes may seem familiar to readers of folktales from many different cultures. Indeed, folklore existed long before humanity divided itself into nations, and the free exchange among cultures has meant that folktales from around the world often bear striking resemblance to one another. What, then, makes Vietnamese folklore particularly Vietnamese? The folklorist Nguyen Dong Chi answered that question by determining four distinctive features of Vietnamese folktales:

1. The imaginative elements of Vietnamese folktales do not stray far from reality. Supernatural events and characters are rare, and usually appear in skillful combination with more realistic ones.
2. Vietnamese folklore originates from the social systems of an Eastern monarchical society, and uses the model of the village as a foundation. The stories are notable for their elegant balance, gentleness, and humanity.

3. The protagonists in Vietnamese folktales often display dissatisfaction with the state of the world. They aim toward a new society that is more just and more reasonable.
4. Many stories mention the active role of women, often reflecting a desire for more freedom in love and marriage.

Although all of these features raise interesting issues about Vietnamese folklore and the nature of Vietnamese society, we will focus here on the first feature because of the ways in which it highlights the development of Vietnamese folklore in general. Unlike the folklore of many other nations, Vietnamese stories do not rely heavily on the supernatural. Many of these stories do contain unbelievable elements—a magic golden tortoise gives lessons to a king, a mandarin's daughter sees the face of a poor fisherman in her cup of tea—but their most essential qualities are realistic. For example, although the poor woodcutter Thach Sanh battles ferocious otherworldly beings and even visits the realm of the Emperor of the Ocean, the heart of his story lies in his relationship with Ly Thong, an evil but very human foe.

This reliance on naturalistic elements is most likely a result of the stories' evolution. In its early development, Vietnamese folklore probably mirrored that of many other ancient cultures. Traditionally, individual cultures have used folklore as a way of explaining natural phenomena. Through extraordinary imagery and exaggerated renditions of human prowess, early folklore created a world that was both separate from and inextricably tied to the world in which human beings really lived. Folktales reflected the psychology of a people who were both afraid of nature and charmed by it.

As early societies developed, people became less dependent upon the vagaries of nature and more likely to distinguish between the reality of the natural world and the imaginary qualities of their stories, a transition that we could describe as a shift from "God's comedy and tragedy" to "humanity's comedy and tragedy." Although early cultures still habitually relied on myth, folktales evolved in such a way that the folk characters often lost their strange and barbarous attributes and became more human. It's impossible to state for certain why such an evolution might have taken place, but factors most likely include the natural social changes within families, the break down of traditions, and conflicts between clans, communes, and different national and ethnic groups. Any of these changes could contribute to the shift from a heavily mythologized folklore to one with a greater reliance on stories of daily life. As such stories evolved, mythologic elements became less important as an explanation for the cosmos than as a means of stimulating the enjoyment of the story and satisfying fantasies about a dangerous world that humans would like to conquer. It's important to remember, however, that the evolution of these folktales occurred very slowly, not over years but over generations and centuries, and while individual stories might have changed dramatically, they managed to retain particular qualities that made them unique.

Vietnamese folklore most likely lost its heavy reliance on myth for many of the reasons stated above, but this change also occurred as a result of political, social, religious, and cultural factors that were peculiar to Vietnam. In terms of folklore, it's helpful to divide Vietnamese history into two distinct periods. The first begins in the Dong Son period, with the historically based myths of the Hung Kings, whom the Vietnamese consider their first leaders, and continues through the initial Chinese invasion of 111 B.C. and the subsequent 1,049 years of Chinese domination, which ended in 938 A.D.[1] The second period begins in 938 A.D., when the victory of Viet leader Ngo Quyen over the Nam Han (the Chinese) established an independent nation known as Dai Viet. During the millennium of Chinese domination, with its highly organized society, the habitual life of the Vietnamese people, who still operated on a tribal level at that time, was turned upside down. As a result, the myths and legends that contained the culture's belief system, with its numerous festivals, witchcraft, religious traditions, and social customs—glimpses of which can still be seen in the fabulous archaeological relics of the Dong Son period—were forbidden and destroyed through the process of forced acculturation into Chinese civilization. Few folktales survived that bear the characteristics of their original Vietnamese forms, and they seem to lack thematic or historical coherence.[2]

Before 1945, 95 percent of Vietnamese were illiterate. Vietnamese folklore existed orally, within the consciousness and subconsciousness of the culture. Because the stories were passed along from person to person, they were not dependent on the written character system, and this independence helped in some ways to ensure their survival. But the overreliance on oral tradition also left the folklore vulnerable to social and political change, change that continued well into the period of independence from the Chinese colonizers. For example, under the Tran Dynasty (1226–1400 A.D.), the monarchy instituted political reforms modeled on the Chinese system. As part of that reform, temples and shrines dedicated to the worship of folk beliefs, rather than Buddhist ones, were considered "illicit" and therefore destroyed. These policies contributed to the loss of the myths and legends based on the concepts of *phon thuc*, a form of fertility worship that was widely followed among the wet-rice cultures of Southeast Asia. During subsequent dynasties, Confucianism replaced Buddhism and continued the task of "reforming superstition." By replacing folk beliefs with such Confucian ethics as "loyalty, filial piety, virtue, and charity" and "the three bonds and the five constants,"[3] authorities believed that they were taming the nation of its primitive habits and customs. Folktales that seemed strange or somehow incongruous within the new Confucian system were altered and put into a historical context, using the new moral standards to give the stories a "clean and beautiful" background.[4]

For example, during the reign of Quang Thieu (1516–1522 A.D.), a mandarin named Nguyen Binh re-edited the genealogies of various village spirits using the Confucian formula. These edited versions excised many of the rich details and artistically complicated plots that originally belonged to the stories. Characters who seemed too "primitive" were made to appear more up-to-date. Mythical exaggerations and illogical details—the most distinctive feature of myths—were changed in order to become smooth and reasonable stories that could illustrate moral and practical lessons for later generations. As the folklorist Nguyen Dong Chi put it, "One may recognize a principle in the development of Vietnamese folktales: the mythical, incredible, and miraculous elements of folktales decrease proportionate to the community's increasing awareness of reason and consciousness of its place in time."[5]

Despite such forced alterations over the years, Vietnamese folklore remains uniquely Vietnamese. While the simplicity and lack of exaggeration of Vietnamese folktales probably resulted from the historical factors of forced acculturation and authoritarian revision, the style also closely mirrors primary Vietnamese values, namely, "Don't stray far from earthly reason" and "Do things in moderation." Even stories that seem clearly to have been imported from other cultures take on a more logical slant in the Vietnamese version. As the scholars of Vietnamese culture Maurice M. Durand and

Nguyen Tran Huan explain it, "In the way that miracles mix with reality, we can clearly see the ways in which the Vietnamese spirit refuses to determine a border between the real and the supernatural. Here, historical events mix with stories about ghosts and miracles, and the world of illusion is closely attached to the world of human beings."[6] Indeed, the values of practicality and humanism lie at the heart of these folktales, and, to the extent that they mix miraculous elements with more realistic ones, the supernatural details always serve the purpose of the human dramas.

Meanings and Ideologies
of the Folktales in this Book

A Daughter's Love

Vietnamese folklore often mixes historical reality and myth without attempting to distinguish between the two. "A Daughter's Love" is a good example of that tendency. Scholars have been able to trace the character of Trieu Da to a real person, an ethnic Chinese leader who had his capital in Phien Ngung, now known as Guangzhou, China. This leader divided the kingdom of Au Lac, which is in the north of modern-day Vietnam, into the two districts of Giao Chi and Cuu Chan. As for the character of An Duong Vuong, no one knows for sure if such a person ever existed. However, the story raises two issues that have plagued actual Viet leaders throughout history: first, the tricky problems of alliance among tribes and, second, the importance of self-defense and the prevention of invasion by enemies from the north. On the most obvious level, one can read the story as a lesson in keeping one's guard up. An Duong Vuong's mistake lies in the fact that he built a strong rampart to keep out the enemy, but failed to see that the enemy was inside his house, right behind him. However, Vietnamese generally take a more generous view of the story, focusing less on the mistakes of battle than on the tragedies of love. Violence destroys the sincere and pure bond between Mi Chau and Trong Thuy. Although both of these lovers committed acts of betrayal, the truly guilty are those who persist in war, not those who love without calculation. In a perfect symbol of the endurance of love, and the resilience of art, the water from the well, the incarnation of Trong Thuy, brightens the pearl, the incarnation of Mi Chau.

The Anger of the Waters
Throughout Southeast Asia, where land and water are the essential ingredients for the sustenance of an agricultural society, "Land" and "Water" play important roles within an ideology known as "dual cosmos," which dictates that life exists through the competing powers of opposing forces. Within Vietnamese ideology in particular, this dual way of thinking expresses itself in opposites, often used symbolically in religion and art. The decorative designs on the Dong Son drums (circa 500 B.C.), for example, show a variety of opposing forms: Bird/Deer, Fish/Crocodile, Male/Female. In another example, the myth of the creation of the Viet nation describes the union of Lac Long Quan, the Father Dragon, who comes from the water, and Au Co, the Mother Bird (or Fairy), who comes from the sky. Following their union, Lac Long takes fifty sons back to the ocean, while Au Co carries fifty sons back to the mountain. Seen symbolically, the story expresses both the conflict between and the harmony among opposing elements. In the story "The Anger of the Waters," this dualism manifests itself in the battle between Son Tinh, the God of the Mountain, and Thuy Tinh, the God of the Water, for the hand of the princess Mi Nuong. This story remains so important within Vietnamese culture that people continue to

worship Son Tinh's Tan Vien Mountain (the actual Ba Vi Mountain, 40 kilometers west of Hanoi) as the Ancestor Mountain.

The Golden Voice

Although "The Golden Voice" is rather typical in its highly romantic and lyrical depiction of love, it also presents surprisingly complicated characters and a sophisticated assessment of conflict between classes. Mi Nuong, the daughter of the mandarin who rules the province, falls in love with the poor fisherman Truong Chi because of the lovely sound of his voice. Pining for him, she becomes sick. When she finally sees him, however, she falls out of love and regains her health. Truong Chi, on the other hand, doesn't love Mi Nuong until the moment he sees her and, aware of the hopelessness of that love, dies of a broken heart. The ease and superficiality of Mi Nuong's affection contrasts sharply with the deeply felt, and fatal, emotions suffered by Truong Chi. Although Truong Chi dies, the very end of the story is, according to Vietnamese thinking, somewhat liberating. Mi Nuong's regret, which leads to the breaking of the cup, releases Truong Chi's spirit to Heaven.

Princess Lieu Hanh, Tea-Seller of Ngang Mountain

Some of the most impressive women in Vietnamese folklore, like the Trung Sisters and Lady Trieu, are based on authentic figures in Vietnamese history. However, the presentation of these actual women lost much rich detail during the Confucian period, when scholars modified the stories to make them more moralistic or purely historical. In contrast, mythic female characters remain vivid and enticing, often more attractive to the imagination than the authentic women. Somehow, perhaps because of the obviously fantastic nature of such stories, Confucian ideologues seem to have ignored them, leaving a space within Vietnamese folklore for complex characters with strong and vibrant personalities. The character of Lieu Hanh, who certainly belongs among this group of mythic women, is noteworthy for her stubbornness, rebelliousness, and lack of restraint. In her defiance of men in general and her father in particular, she not only violates the established codes of female conduct, but seems to relish doing so. Although the other characters in Lieu Hanh's story, and the folktale's audience in real life, may criticize her behavior, it is also compelling enough to make her a fascinating and popular figure. This paradox—the fact that Lieu Hanh both attracts and repels—occurs with some frequency among the mythical females in Vietnamese folklore. Seen as both fairies and ghosts, both benign and malevolent, these highly complicated women speak to a desire among common people for greater freedom in their own lives. At the conclusions of these stories of fantastic women, they always migrate to the world of the spirit. In a sense, these transformations help to bridge the gap between the natural and the supernatural, between humanity and the world of the spirits.

The Infant General of Phu Dong Village

Vietnamese worship a pantheon of four immortal Gods: Son Tinh, the god of Tan Vien Mountain; Saint Giong, the infant general of Phu Dong village; Chu Dao Tu (also known as Chu Dong Tu); and, the Mother Fairy, Lieu Hanh. Of these four immortals, Saint Giong represents the ideological national hero who sets the example for all subsequent defenders of the nation. Every year, the Viet people throw a lavish celebration to remember the miracle in which the nation, with the help of Saint Giong, defended itself from foreign invaders. During this ritual, they praise the image of the infant who never talks or smiles or grows, but responds immediately to the call to defend the nation, stretching his shoulders to become a giant, bowing to his mother, and going off to the battlefield to fight for independence. After his victory, this hero takes off his armor and rides his horse into the sky, never even acknowledging the fortune offered by the king. Vietnamese admire such selflessness, this tendency to be disinterested and to withdraw when one's work is done. Vietnamese folklore reflects that philosophy in Saint Giong's response to the call of his country without any expectation of personal reward.

Three Drops of Blood

This story, which bears the dogmatic hallmarks of Confucianism in decline, may have come into existence much later than the others. The obvious moral lesson of the story condemns ingratitude and promotes faithfulness and virtue in women. Still, the malleability of folktales makes it possible to read other meanings into the plot. For example, the story might also stand as a comment on the ways in which an authoritarian and despotic society makes women faithless and cruel. Vietnamese culture, indeed, reflects such contradictions. While the strict standards of Confucianism require women to abide by "the three submissions and the four virtues,"[7] Vietnamese folk culture coined the phrase, "Wife first, then Heaven."

The Toad Is the Uncle of the King of Heaven

In comparison to that of other nations, the folklore of Vietnam does not contain many stories about animals. It's possible that some such stories were lost. However, reason plays a very strong role in Vietnamese thinking about spiritual matters, and it may have deterred people from looking for purely symbolic images in the creation of folktales. In this rare case of an animal as a protagonist in a folktale, however, it's not surprising that the Vietnamese turned to the toad. The popularity of the toad within Vietnamese culture can be documented as far back as the Dong Son period, during which time images of the amphibian appeared on many drums. As the folktale demonstrates, wet-rice farmers of Vietnam have long valued the creature because of its perceived link to rain. The purple toad, in particular, symbolizes success and power. The Vietnamese folk image of a young boy hugging a toad is so popular that people hang it in their homes as a way to wish for prosperity. And one folk medicine utilizes the meat of the toad, particularly for children, because of its supposed healthful properties.

Two Cakes Fit for a King
The story "Two Cakes Fit for a King" explains the Vietnamese tradition of serving two cakes, the round *giay* and the square *chung*, to worship Heaven and Earth on the occasion of the Lunar New Year. Not only does the story explain the historical background of a ritual, however, it also helps explain the basic concepts of Vietnamese thinking regarding the structure of the cosmos. As in "The Anger of the Waters," the story presents a dualistic view of the universe that was common among ancient Vietnamese and continues to influence thinking today. Here, the round cake symbolizes Heaven, the creator, whereas the square cake symbolizes the Earth, the creation. Often, the round shape becomes attached to the idea of a God, looking down at the square shape, the Earth. Once again, the ideology produces a pairing of opposites: round and square, continuity and discontinuity, creator and creation, supernatural and natural, Heaven and Earth.

The Story of Watermelon Island

Some Vietnamese folktales appear to idealize religion, promoting a "leave-this-world-of-dust" philosophy. But, taking a look at such stories from the perspective of folk philosophy, they also seem to carry healthy, nonreligious, practical ideals. "The Story of Watermelon Island" is a good example of such a story. Several aspects of the story point to a foundation in Buddhist thinking. Mai An Tiem, the orphan boy brought up by the king, arrives on a trade ship, most likely from India or Turkey, two nations that had early trading histories along the Vietnamese coast. The boy's origins are significant in that they hint at the import of Buddhism into Vietnam from India. In fact, the ancient Vietnamese word for "watermelon," *tay qua*, means, literally, the melon that came from the West. For Vietnamese in centuries past, the term "West" denoted the birthplace of the Boddhisatva and also the location of Nirvana. In addition, Mai An Tiem's saying that "Wealth doesn't matter" hints at Buddhist teachings. On the other hand, these references to Buddhist philosophy may be less important in themselves than as a means of challenging certain concepts of "royal power" within Eastern monarchical society. On the whole, the world view of folk Vietnamese centers not on Buddhist philosophy but on a patriarchal peasant society centered within the life of the village. The isolated nature of that society guarantees the peculiar strengths and limitations of the rural Vietnamese world view, which focuses on material concerns over complicated systems of religion or ideological orthodoxy. Differences between Buddhist, Confucian, and folk thinking become very clear in the sort of reasoning particular to each ideology. A Buddhist will talk about "detachment." A Confucian will talk about "the king and his subjects." A common person will say,

"Heaven gives birth to elephants, and heaven will provide them grass."

Thach Sanh

In both motif and detail, this story repeats a popular feature of many international folktales: the story of an ideologic hero of the common people. In fact, "Thach Sanh" is so close to some Indian folktales that it might indeed have originated there. The folklore scholar Stith Thompson, in the *Motif-Index to Folk Literature*, traces the origins of many Vietnamese folktales back to India. Given the centuries of political, social, and cultural exchange between Vietnam and China, it's somewhat surprising that India, rather than China, would play such a prominent role in Vietnamese folklore. However, Indian stories may have been introduced into Vietnam through the culture of Champa, a pre-modern Indianized kingdom that was conquered by the Vietnamese as they moved south to expand their territory. The image of a fire-breathing snake, and fire-worship in general, appear in ancient Indian folktales as well as in ancient Indian religious customs and habits. However, the tale of a poor man overcoming adversity and earning the respect of his people can no doubt be found in many different cultures, and it would be impossible to pin down the origins of a story that varies so widely, even in Vietnam.[8] Perhaps more interesting is the fact that one element of the story does seems particular to the Vietnamese versions, and is particularly Vietnamese. That is the presence of a small musical instrument—in this case, the lute. The notes of the lute float through the walls of the palace and awaken the heart of the princess. The notes of the lute lull the spirits of the enemy soldiers and convince them not to fight. This tiny instrument, both insignificant and powerful, serves as a compelling symbol to a nation that sees itself as continually struggling for its own survival.

A Note on the Illustrations by Bui Hoai Mai

Unlike in the West, the traditions of Vietnamese art have not focused on the talents of individuals. The French opened Vietnam's first professional art training school in Hanoi in 1925, and that for the purpose of training local artisans to supply fine art products for the markets back in Europe. Up until that time, Vietnamese artists never even had a tradition of signing their names to their work. However, it would be a mistake to think that Vietnamese did not care about art. In fact, Vietnam has a long tradition of fine art, one that is based not on academies or personal reputations but on the communal life of each individual village.

Considering the size of most Vietnamese villages, and the relative lack of wealth there, these communities have produced an astonishing amount of art. For example, in the nineteenth century, 300 to 500 people inhabited a typical village in the Red River Delta. Most villages would have a pagoda, a communal house, and several shrines where the daily activities of spiritual life occurred. Each pagoda or communal house would possess several dozen statues, both small and large, and the buildings themselves contained elaborate architectural detail and splendid red and gold ornamentation. Here in the heart of folk culture, not in museums or the rarefied collections of royal families, Vietnam's fine art heritage has thrived. This fact makes sense in the context of Vietnamese thinking about art and its purpose. Rather than keeping art separate from daily life, Vietnamese prefer to blend the two together. In order to understand Vietnamese fine art, one must begin, then, with folk art: literature, music, crafts, painting, sculpture, festivals, beliefs, even customs and habits.

Creating the illustrations for this book gave me the opportunity to re-experience my childhood, much of which I spent living in a village in Northern Vietnam. I devised the style of the images by combining two types of art that remain popular in rural culture. The first, Dong Ho and Hang Trong folk painting, appeared before the seventeenth century, around the time that Vietnamese villages became more developed and stable. Dong Ho artwork, a type of wood-cut painting, originated in Ho village in what is now known as Bac Ninh Province. Villagers would both farm and produce the paintings, which they then sold in the markets on the occasion of Tet, the Lunar New Year. Often, the paintings contained images that could be read as wishes for good luck in the coming year. Other topics focused on images and activities of the countryside: chickens, pigs, lute-playing on the back of a water buffalo, battles between rivals in love, and festival customs. Artists created the paintings using natural colors on *do* paper, a paper made from the bark of the *do* tree, using a foundation of *diep*, a powder made from grinding the glittery shells of oysters. Although Dong Ho artwork came from the countryside, Hang Trong painting developed on Hang Trong and Hang Non Streets in the heart of Hanoi. Artists produced these paintings by first drawing black outlines and then coloring the pictures by hand. Hang Trong paintings reflect a more urban aesthetic, and the subject matter is more spiritual. For example, some popular motifs include such religious imagery as the Five Tigers, the Virgin Girl, the Carp Looking at the Moon, and the Three Altars of the Mother Goddess.

In addition to drawing from these two popular styles of folk painting, I also took inspiration from the imagery of nature and daily life that one finds engraved in the vertical and horizontal wooden pillars of village communal houses. Here, in these simple images, one can clearly see the ways in which life penetrates art, freeing art from the conventional standards of form and content. By using folk materials, folk techniques, and folk imagery, I hope to bring that sense of mixing art and life to the readers of these folktales.

Notes

1. The Pre-Dong Son periods and the Dong Son period formed the historical foundation of the Viet nation. It's very difficult to date ancient Vietnamese history exactly. However, scholars organize the Pre-Dong Son periods into the Phung Nguyen Culture (2000–1500 B.C.), the Dong Dau Culture (1500–1100 B.C.), and the Go Mun Culture (1100–700 B.C.). The Dong Son period is estimated to have existed from 700 B.C. to 100 A.D.

2. "Those folktales that did survive are found in the writings of the Vietnamese during medieval times. They have also been found in the epic myths of the Muong minority people." *Lich Su Tu Tuong Viet Nam, Tap 1.*

3. The three bonds are king/subject, father/son, and husband/wife. The five constants are benevolence, righteousness, propriety, knowledge, and sincerity.

4. Confucianism is based on the thinking of Confucious (551–479 B.C.), a great teacher of ancient China. Through twenty-five centuries of development, Confucianism has changed considerably. In the early years, it was neither a religion nor a philosophy, but a moral and political theory adopted by the Chinese ruling classes.

5. Nguyen Dong Chi.

6. Maurice M. Durand and Nguyen Tran Huan.

7. The Three Submissions refers to the three men to whom a woman must submit: her father, her husband, and, after her husband dies, her son. The Four Virtues refer to domestic labor, appearance, speech, and conduct.

8. In one version, Thach Sanh is a person of Khmer, rather than Vietnamese, origin. In another version, Thach Sanh's homeland is in Cao Bang, in the north of Vietnam.

References

Chevalier, Jean and Alain Gheerbrant. *Tu dien Bieu tuong van hoa the gioi* [Dictionary of Cultural Symbols in the World]. Danang: Danang Publishing House, Nguyen Du Writing Academy, 1997, p. 202 (Vietnamese Translation).

Condominas, Georges. *Khong gian xa hoi vung Dong Nam A* [Social Space in Southeast Asia]. Hanoi: Culture Publishing House, 1997 (Vietnamese Translation).

Durand, Maurice M. and Nguyen Huan Tran. *An Introduction to Vietnamese Literature.* New York: Columbia University Press, 1985, p. 14 (Vietnamese Translation).

Huynh Ly and Nguyen Xuan Lan, editors. *Truyen Thach Sanh* [The Story of Thach Sanh]. Hanoi: Literature Publishing House, 1971.

Nguyen Duy Hinh. *Tin nguong thanh hoang lang Viet Nam* [Beliefs about Village Gods in Vietnamese Villages]. Hanoi: The Social Sciences Publishing House, 1996, p. 392.

Nguyen Dang Thuc. *Lich su tu tuong Viet Nam—Tap 1: Tu tuong binh dan Viet Nam* [The History of Vietnamese Ideology—Volume 1: Vietnamese Folk Ideology]. Ho Chi Minh City: Ho Chi Minh City Publishing House, 1992, p. 185, 203, 217, 283.

Nguyen Dong Chi. *Kho tang truyen co tich Viet Nam: 2 tap* [The Treasury of Vietnamese Folktales: Two Volumes]. Hanoi: Education Publishing House, 2000, p. 1587–1705.

Nguyen Dong Chi. *Luoc khao ve than thoai Viet Nam—Tai lieu tham khao van hoc—in lan thu hai* [A Summary of Vietnamese Myth, Literary Referential Documents, Second Edition]. Hanoi: Literature, History, and Geography Publishing House, 1956.

Nguyen Phan Quang and Vo Xuan Dan. *Lich su Viet Nam tu nguon goc den nam 1884* [Vietnamese History from the Origin to the Year 1884]. Ho Chi Minh City: Ho Chi Minh City Publishing House, 2000.

Nguyen Thai Thu (editor), Phan Dai Doan, Nguyen Duc Su, and Ha Van Tan. *Lich su tu tuong Viet Nam—tap 1* [The History of Vietnamese Ideology—Volume 1]. Vietnamese Institute of Sociology and Vietnamese Institute of Philosophy. Hanoi: The Social Sciences Publishing House, 1993, p. 63–64.

Thompson, Stith. *Motif-Index of Folk-Literature: A Classification of Narrative Elements in Folk Tales, Ballads, Myths, Fables, Mediaeval Romances, Exampla, Fabliaux, Jest-Books, and Local Legends.* Bloomington: Indiana University Press, 1955.

Tran Quoc Vuong. *Van hoa Viet Nam tim toi va suy ngam* [Searching For and Thinking about Vietnamese Culture]. Hanoi: Ethnic Culture Publishing House; *Culture and Art Magazine*, 2000, p. 234.

Tylor, Edward. *The Origins of Primitive Culture: Religion in Primitive Culture.* Hanoi: Ethnic Culture Publishing House; *Culture and Art Magazine*, 2001, p. 422 (Vietnamese Translation).

Various authors. *Hung Vuong dung nuoc* [The Hung Kings Built the Country]. Hanoi: The Social Sciences Publishing House, 1972.

A Daughter's Love

ᕱᕱᕱᕱᕱᕱᕱᕱᕱᕱᕱᕱᕱᕱᕱᕱᕱᕱᕱᕱ

Long ago, Au Lac's king, An Duong Vuong, ordered his subjects to build a large and solid rampart surrounded by a deep trench, to protect the tiny nation from invasion.

An Duong Vuong expected the rampart to be magnificent, but before the work was half complete, something very strange and terrible happened. The king and his subjects woke one morning to find that all the work they had accomplished the day before had somehow been destroyed during the night.

That evening, the king ordered 100 of his brightest soldiers to stay awake to catch the culprit. From sunset to sunrise, none of them so much as blinked an eye. But they saw nothing, and the next morning, the king awoke again to find that some mysterious spirit had destroyed all the previous day's work in the night.

At this rate, the rampart would never be completed, and Au Lac would always face the fear of invasion. An Duong Vuong decided to watch the place himself. That night he didn't sleep at all, but he, too, discovered nothing. The next morning, as before, everything they had accomplished lay in ruins.

The king was full of sorrow. How could he protect his people if he couldn't even complete the rampart to defend them? In desperation, he built an altar to pray to Heaven and Earth and to call for the help of the Gods. For many days he stayed in this shrine, hoping that by renouncing the luxuries of his royal life he could prove his true and faithful heart. The king's wife had died, and the only person he would see during this time of prayer was Mi Chau,[1] his only daughter. She cooked her father's simple meals of rice and vegetables, and she washed his tattered beggar's clothes.

One night during this period, the king had a dream. An angel appeared in the form of a golden turtle and said to him, "I am Kim Quy Divine. I am moved by your prayers, and I will help you in your wish to protect your people. You are right to build a rampart, but the shape is wrong. Build a rampart that wraps into itself like a snail's shell, and you will be able to finish it soon." Then Kim Quy disappeared and the king woke up. Before the sun rose over the distant mountains, the people of Au Lac had already begun work on the new rampart, following the golden turtle's advice exactly.

Just as the turtle had promised, one month later the rampart, called Loa Thanh, was complete. No one, not even the most ancient woman in the kingdom, who was over 130 years old, had ever seen such a solid, imposing structure. The rampart walls curled into themselves like the shell of a snail, and no invaders could figure out how to get inside.

An Duong Vuong returned to royal life and held a great feast to thank Kim Quy Divine. That night, the golden turtle appeared to the king in another dream. Handing the king one of its golden claws, the turtle said, "Now I offer you this gift to defend your territory. Make a bow's trigger out of it, and you'll have a miraculous weapon. This bow will never miss its mark, and it will kill thousands of enemy soldiers with every shot. But I also have one word of warning. Keep the golden claw very carefully. If you lose it, you will lose your country!" With that advice, the turtle disappeared.

The king woke up and found the claw at his side. He picked it up carefully and called his most skillful bowmaker to construct the bow. Nine days later, the bowmaker presented the king with the weapon, which shone like the moon and was so big that only the strongest soldiers could lift it. An Duong Vuong kept the precious gift next to his bed.

At that time, Au Lac's worst enemy was the country of Nam Hai, which is now a part of southern China. Year after year, the king of Nam Hai invaded, but An Duong Vuong used his divine bow to defeat the enemy every time.

The king of Nam Hai, Trieu Da, was a clever man. Although he knew nothing of the golden bow, he realized that in order to win Au Lac he would have to find a way other than military force. He wanted to discover An Duong Vuong's secret strength and destroy it. For that purpose, he came up with a plan.

Trieu Da sent a peace delegation to Au Lac, at the head of which was his only son, Trong Thuy. Trong Thuy carried a message from his father suggesting that the two countries cement their new alliance of friendship through marriage. Trieu Da proposed that his son should take the hand of Mi Chau, King An Duong Vuong's daughter.

King An Duong Vuong was glad to establish peace with his former enemy. He was not yet willing to agree to the plan of marriage, but he welcomed Trong Thuy into the palace.

In those days, love never played a major role in the marriage plans of princes and princesses. Rather, kings used the hands of their children to strengthen their own positions of power. The relationship between Trong Thuy and Mi Chau was special from the start, though. Trong Thuy was instantly moved by the divine beauty of the princess, and Mi Chau could not fail to notice the handsome young man. In addition, Mi Chau played the lute more exquisitely than the finest musicians Trong Thuy had ever heard, and when the prince sang to accompany her, the lovely tones of his voice moved Mi Chau to tears.

Trong Thuy hadn't even been at the palace a month before the love between the two young people became apparent to everyone. Even the king enjoyed the sight of the happy couple talking for hours while they sat on a large white rock in the palace garden. King An Duong Vuong didn't feel suspicious at all when he saw his daughter and the son of his former enemy wandering through the secret passages of the rampart. Recognizing the love between the two young people, he agreed to let Mi Chau marry the Nam Hai prince.

The couple lived in harmony, playing chess, reciting poems, and spending quiet afternoons admiring the beautiful flowers in the palace gardens. Day after day, night after night, their life passed in peace and serenity. Mi Chau was so happy, she thought that life would always be this way.

One night, when the moon was very bright and the stars flickered like diamonds in the sky, Mi Chau and Trong Thuy were sitting on the big rock in the garden, looking out over the high rampart. They had been there a long time when a cold wind suddenly blew through the trees. Large white clouds began to roll across the sky.

Mi Chau started to shiver, and Trong Thuy pulled her closer to him. Then he whispered, "My darling, now we are as dear to each other as two people can ever be. We must always be truthful with one another, and so I want to ask you something. Is there a secret reason why your father's kingdom has never been defeated?"

Mi Chau turned to her husband and said, "There's no

secret, my love! Au Lac has a high, strong rampart and a deep trench. It also has a divine bow that can kill thousands of enemy soldiers with every shot. How could anyone defeat us?"

Trong Thuy asked Mi Chau many questions about the bow, and she finally led her husband to the king's bedroom so that Trong Thuy could see it for himself. Even in the dark night, the golden claw glowed as if it were imbued with light. As Mi Chau explained to Trong Thuy how to use the bow, Trong Thuy listened quietly, looking closely at the trigger and at the particular size and shape of the instrument. Then the young couple put the bow back in its place and went back to their own quarters to sleep.

The next morning, Trong Thuy asked for An Duong Vuong's permission to go back to Nam Hai to visit his father, Trieu Da. Within a few days, the young prince was telling his father the whole story of the divine bow. Trieu Da was thrilled with the information and ordered his servants to make a false trigger out of the claw of an ordinary turtle, which would look exactly like King An Duong Vuong's magical trigger. Trong Thuy then hid the new trigger in his clothes and returned with it to Au Lac.

An Duong Vuong held a huge party to welcome his son-in-law home. At the party, Trong Thuy held up his glass of wine and offered toast after toast to his new family. An Duong Vuong and Mi Chau drank many glasses of wine, but Trong Thuy himself drank only a little. Soon the king and Mi Chau were fast asleep. Trong Thuy sneaked into the king's bedroom, stole the golden trigger, and replaced it with his false one.

The next morning, Mi Chau thought her husband seemed worried and restless. "What is bothering you, my darling?" she asked.

Trong Thuy looked at his wife and said, "I have to leave.

My royal father has told me that I must return to Nam Hai immediately so that I can accompany him to battle very far away in the north. It's possible that I will be gone a long time."

Mi Chau looked at the ground and said nothing. Trong Thuy took her hand and continued, "I have no idea when we will meet again, my love, but I know that we will. We must think of a way to find each other, because if there is a war, you may have to leave this place. I can't live without you, and so I have to know how to find you."

For several moments, Mi Chau said nothing. Then finally she whispered, "I have a goose-feather coat. Wherever I go, I will drop feathers along my way. You can follow that trail of feathers to find me."

Trong Thuy was pale now. He knew that if he didn't leave quickly, he would never be able to leave at all. The young lovers hugged each other. Neither one could even speak. Then Trong Thuy gathered his things and left. For a long time, My Chau stood by the window staring down at the garden below her, the tears streaming down her cheek.

Back in Nam Hai, Trong Thuy gave his father the golden claw. Trieu Da held the magic trigger in his hands and proclaimed, "This time, Au Lac will be mine!" Trong Thuy said nothing. He simply turned and walked away. A few days later, he and his father led the entire military force of Nam Hai across the border and into the kingdom of Au Lac.

When An Duong Vuong heard that Nam Hai had invaded his kingdom, he swore at King Trieu Da's deceit. However, trusting the power of his divine bow, he made no preparation for battle. Not until the enemy had nearly reached the rampart did he pull out his precious weapon and shoot. It was only at that moment, when the shot failed to have its magical effect, that the king realized the depth of his misfortune.

The Nam Hai soldiers rushed the rampart gates. Within

minutes, the solid walls began to crumble. An Duong Vuong pulled Mi Chau up onto his horse with him, and they escaped through the back gate. From her seat on the galloping horse, Mi Chau plucked goose feathers out of her coat, and left a trail so that her husband could find her.

The mountain roads were rough and dangerous. For several days, their horse ran without rest. Finally, late one afternoon, the road climbed Da Son Mountain and led to a cliff overlooking the Eastern Sea. The king and the princess stopped and got off the horse. An Duong Vuong looked at the sun setting over the horizon and realized he was trapped. Although the road continued along the edge of the cliff, it was too narrow to travel at night. At the same time, they couldn't rest or turn back, because the enemy troops might be right behind them.

An Duong Vuong knelt down and whispered the name of Kim Quy Divine. Suddenly, the wind picked up, blowing sand and dirt in all directions, shaking the leaves, shaking the trees, shaking the whole mountain. Then the clear image of the golden turtle appeared within the fog of dust. "The enemy," the turtle said, "is at your back." With that, Kim Quy disappeared.

King An Duong Vuong looked around. In the fading light, he saw the trail of feathers on the ground behind them. Now he knew the truth. Without another thought, he took out his sword. Mi Chau closed her eyes. Then, with one fatal stroke, King An Duong Vuong cut off his daughter's head. He stood for a moment, looking down at the body of his precious child, then he hurled himself over the cliff and into the sea.

Back at the capital, Trieu Da's soldiers had taken over the whole Loa Thanh rampart. As soon as he saw that the battle was over, Trong Thuy got on his horse and rushed off to find his love. For days, he followed the trail of feathers, through forest and hills, then up into the mountains until he finally reached Da Son Mountain at the edge of the sea. There, beside the cliff, lay the body of Mi Chau. Trong Thuy fell to his knees and covered his face in his hands.

Two days later, Trieu Da, his soldiers, and all the people of Loa Thanh saw Trong Thuy riding slowly back to the rampart with the body of Mi Chau. Although his father and all his friends tried to get the young man to speak, he said nothing, and he wouldn't allow anyone to go near the body of his beloved wife. Silently, he buried her beside the white rock where the two lovers had always sat looking at the stars. Then, before anyone could stop him, he threw himself into the palace well and drowned.

Nowadays, at Co Loa village just outside Hanoi, the well called Trong Thuy sits in front of An Duong Vuong's temple. According to Vietnamese legend, when the king killed his daughter, her blood flowed into the sea. Oysters drank those drops of blood and produced pearls that were large, but glowed only dimly. Local people say that if the pearls are washed in the water of Trong Thuy's well, they will shine with a translucence as bright and beautiful as the moon.

The contemporary Vietnamese poet Anh Ngoc wrote a poem that recalls the tragedy of Mi Chau and Trong Thuy:

> *Tears become the other side of trust*
> *Ultimately love is death*
> *But the beautiful girl, even headless, still has beauty*
> *And love, even with betrayal, is still love.*

Note

1. Many Vietnamese folktales contain young women by the name of Mi Chau or Mi Nuong. These are honorary titles given to the daughters of high-ranking officials, similar to "princess" in English.

The Anger of the Waters

A LONG TIME AGO, the land we now know as Vietnam was governed by a series of rulers known as the Hung Kings. During the dynasty of the Eighteenth Hung King, the Viet people lived in peace and happiness.

The king lived with one sorrow. His wife had died young, leaving the heartbroken husband to raise their little girl. Although the king had a palace full of diamonds and pearls, his daughter was his life's joy. Her name was Mi Nuong, and when she grew up she was so beautiful that no one could see her without falling in love with her. Her skin was as smooth and white as the freshest milk. Her lips were as scarlet as the coral that lies at the depths of the ocean. Her eyes shone like deep, dark velvet, and her hair was as soft as clouds in the sky.

Mi Nuong was not only very beautiful. She was also intelligent and talented. She sang beautifully, and she knew how to play all kinds of musical instruments. She also loved her father dearly, and, understanding his sorrow, she did whatever she could to please him.

Because the king valued his daughter above everything

else, he wanted to find the most handsome, talented, and brave man in the world for her to marry. To find the best husband for Mi Nuong, he decided to organize a competition for all the young men in the kingdom. He told his advisers to spread the news that anyone who wanted to marry the princess should come to the palace to show their skills.

Many young men tried. The king met a hunter who could enter the forest after breakfast and bring home a tiger for lunch. He met a swimmer who could stay under water for three hours at a time. He met a scholar who knew how to recite poetry in seventeen different languages. But the hunter couldn't read, the swimmer was too shy to speak, and the scholar sneezed too much. The king didn't give any of them good marks. He began to worry that he would never find anyone good enough for his daughter. Mi Nuong worried that she would never fall in love.

Then one day, two strangers appeared. The first wore clothes that were green as trees in the middle of summer. In his hand was a bow made of rare wood, and an ivory arrow that bore a hundred feathers from a hundred different forest birds. He bowed to the king and said, "Your Highness, I come from the highest point on Tan Vien Mountain. My name is Son Tinh, and I am the Mountain Divine."

The second visitor wore clothes that were as blue as the ocean glowing in the sun. In his hand was a horn made from the shells of a hundred creatures of the sea. He bowed to the king and said, "Your highness, I come from the deepest depths of the Eastern Sea. My name is Thuy Tinh, and I am the Ocean Divine."

The king felt pleased. He had never seen such impressive-looking fellows. Mi Nuong, hiding behind a curtain, felt her heart quickly beating.

But the king was not the sort of person to go by looks alone.

"Show me your talent!" he said.

The visitor dressed in blue stepped forward and bowed. "Your majesty," he said, "because I'm the Water Divine, I control the ponds, lakes, streams, rivers, seas, and oceans. And, even more important, I also control the sky. Watch what I can do!"

He walked out of the palace and blew his seashell horn. Gray clouds rolled in and within minutes covered the whole sky. A big wind churned through the trees, followed by crashing thunder and cracking lightning. Then the clouds opened up and let loose a torrent of rain. Mi Nuong watched it all from the window of the palace. Everything outside became dark and frightening. Even the palace shook .

Just when it seemed the force of the storm would kill them all, the visitor dressed in green ran out of the palace. Braving the wind and rain, he raised his bow and shot the arrow into the air. The storm immediately stopped, and the sky instantly became clear and blue. Birds sang. The water drops on trees and flowers shone like jade. Mi Nuong smiled. Both men came in and knelt down before King Hung, each proud of his accomplishment.

The king was confused. He could see that both of these men possessed a rare talent. How could he say that one was greater than the other? Finally he found a solution—a good one, according to him.

He gestured for the two young men to get up.

"Both of you," said the king, "are young, handsome, and talented. But I only have one daughter. I have to give you one more test. Tomorrow will be the wedding. Whichever one of you brings your engagement presents here first can marry the princess."

The two young visitors bowed and hurried away. They both knew they had a lot to do by the next morning.

Son Tinh, the Mountain Divine, hurried back to Tan Vien Mountain. He ordered his followers to collect all the treasures of the forest and mountains, including ivory, aloe, muskedeen, rare woods, and precious animals. In addition, Son Tinh found three creatures he knew no one at the palace had ever seen: an elephant with nine tusks, a rooster with nine spurs on its feet, and a pink horse with nine different layers of mane. "These animals," he said, "will delight my lovely bride-to-be."

While Son Tinh was collecting everything from the mountains and forests, Thuy Tinh was busy in the Eastern Sea. In hopes of having Mi Nuong come to live in the sea, Thuy Tinh's subjects offered him such treasures as the most delicate coral, the smoothest turtle shells, and the brightest pearls. In addition, Thuy Tinh found three creatures he knew no one at the palace had ever seen, a sea horse as graceful as a Thoroughbred, a starfish that glowed like a star, and a water dragon whose skin shimmered in all the colors of the rainbow. "These sea creatures," Thuy Tinh said, "will delight my lovely bride-to-be."

Early the next morning, while the sun still shone pale on the palace gate and all the people inside were still sleeping, Son Tinh arrived upon his pink horse with nine manes. The elephant followed, bearing all the treasures of the forest and mountain. With its nine spurs, the rooster knocked at the gate.

As soon as the gate opened, the royal wedding music began. Son Tinh and Mi Nuong took each other's hand, walked to the palace altar, and knelt down to pray. Both of them were happy, and all the people who lived between the palace and Tan Vien Mountain were thrilled with joy. The feast began, and everyone danced to congratulate the happy young couple.

Not ten minutes had passed when Thuy Tinh arrived, bearing the gifts of the sea. You can imagine the disappointment he felt when he realized he'd arrived only ten minutes too late. Seeing Son Tinh and Mi Nuong happily married, he was so furious he decided to get revenge. He gathered his many mysterious powers, and called the clouds, winds, rain, and water to make a flood that would kill everybody, including Mi Nuong and Son Tinh, his rival in love.

Thousands of Thuy Tinh's subjects—huge numbers of turtles, octopus, snakes, and water-ghosts—emerged from the rivers and seas with bloody ideas.

But Son Tinh's followers didn't pause to wait for their deaths. As fast as they could, they cut down trees and threw rocks and soil into the water to keep it from rising and drowning them. The Ocean Divine's soldiers died one after another. At the same time, Son Tinh, with his own mysterious power, made the mountain higher and higher, and kept the people safe.

The higher the water rose, the higher the mountain rose.

Finally, the water soldiers were so exhausted they couldn't fight any more. Reluctantly, Thuy Tinh realized he had to withdraw.

Son Tinh's followers rejoiced. They held parties to celebrate their victory. After that, Son Tinh and Mi Nuong lived a happy life together.

But the ocean god never forgot his great disappointment in love. Once every year, he thinks back on his old hatred, and he causes the waters to rise again and flood. Son Tinh's subjects, who are now the people of Vietnam, developed from that day their traditional ways of fighting the floods. They've built great river banks and dikes so that they can always protect themselves from Thuy Tinh's anger.

The Golden Voice

꧁꧂꧁꧂꧁꧂꧁꧂꧁꧂꧁꧂꧁꧂꧁꧂꧁꧂꧁꧂꧁꧂

Ngay xua co anh Truong Chi
Nguoi thi tham xau, hat thi tham hay.
Long ago lived a man named Truong Chi
He was so ugly, yet his voice was so beautiful.

—Vietnamese Folk Song

O NCE UPON a time, in a far, far away village, there was a young man named Truong Chi. His parents had passed away when he was only twelve. After that, Truong Chi lived alone in a crumbling cottage, the only thing his parents left him. The villagers sympathized with the boy, and several even offered to adopt him, but Truong Chi refused. He wanted to be independent. More important, he didn't want to live far from his parents' tombs because he feared wild animals might dig them up.

Truong Chi lived a hard life. Day after day, he went to the forest to cut firewood and search for wild mushrooms, or he went to the river to fish. Whatever he was able to find or catch, he took to the market and traded for rice and the other things he needed to survive. Because he spent his days working in the sun and the rain, his body remained as thin as the bamboo he collected in the forest. His skin, never protected from the harsh outdoors, grew dark and rough. He was ugly, and he was extremely poor as well. He only had one set of clothes, which he wore all year round, making him look just like a beggar. None of the village girls would go near him.

Despite the difficulties of his life, Truong Chi never felt sad. He accepted his poor but peaceful condition. And he possessed one thing that gave him great joy: Perhaps to compensate for Truong Chi's unlucky childhood, the Creator had offered him a magnificent voice. When Truong Chi sang, the birds in the trees forgot to fly, the fish in the river forgot to swim. Truong Chi's warm, sweet voice made old men feel younger. Middle-aged men felt more energetic. Women were able to relax after a long day of work in the fields and in the kitchens. Young men and young women felt the urgent call of love. Even children became more obedient to their parents. Late in the afternoons, after Truong Chi finished his work, he walked to the bank of the river to watch the sunset and to sing. At that moment, all the creatures and all the villagers stood motionless, straining their ears to listen.

Even though he didn't feel sad, as he grew older, Truong Chi began to have desires. One evening in early autumn, when the leaves were turning bright yellow, when the swallows were flying south, and the moon glowed paler than before, Truong Chi stood on the river bank gazing at the river in the moonlight. At that moment, he experienced the vague sensation that people often experience in the fall. He opened his mouth and started to sing about his longing:

> *Fish in the river swim in pairs*
> *Deer in the forest have friends*
> *But I'm still looking for you*
> *My dream love, where are you?*

That night, the autumn breezes carried Truong Chi's voice very far, past the village and down the river to a place where someone new was listening.

Around a bend in that river sat a giant and majestic castle, the home of the mandarin who ruled the province. He was a rich man, so rich that every bowl and dish in his castle was of the purest gold and the finest jade. The chairs he sat on, the tables he ate at, and the bed he slept in were all made of perfumed wood and engraved with ivory. He had so many soldiers and servants that even his chief butler had trouble keeping track of them. All these people worked constantly to make the mandarin happy. Even the flowers in the garden, all the most rare and lovely species in nature, competed to attract him with their beauty and fragrance.

Wealthy as the mandarin was, he had not always been happy. For many, many years, he had wanted a child but failed to produce one with either his wife or any of his ten concubines. Without an heir, the mandarin was miserable. His wife, too, was miserable. She prayed day and night, visited pagodas near and far, and made many offerings to the Buddha. No one knew for sure if her prayers were heard, but, finally, she became pregnant and gave birth to a baby girl. When the child was born, the mandarin was so happy that he ordered a huge party to which the whole province was invited. He named his daughter Mi Nuong.

Mi Nuong lived a delightful childhood. She ate only especially delicious foods. She wore clothes made from the most delicate and softest fabrics. Unlike other people, she didn't bathe in plain water, but in a fragrant bath of pure milk, which made her skin fresh, smooth, and milky white. Her eyes were as black as fine ebony, her lips red as rubies, and her long hair gave off the sweet scent of roses and of youth. As the years passed, Mi Nuong grew extraordinarily beautiful. Perhaps her beauty came from nature alone, but maybe it also came from the ease and comfort of her life. She had never experienced a moment of sorrow. No one, even her parents, ever denied her a thing. To Mi Nuong, wealth and comfort seemed as normal as the sun and the moon and the cool evening breeze. She had no idea that poverty or ugliness existed.

On this particular evening, Mi Nuong had gone out for a walk in the garden with her favorite maids. The air was serene and filled with the smell of night-blooming flowers. The breeze felt like a feather brushing softly against her cheek. Suddenly, Mi Nuong heard in the wind the melodious voice of a man singing a song about love. The deep passion of the singer pierced Mi Nuong's heart and chilled her. For the first time in Mi Nuong's life, sadness invaded her soul.

Every evening after that, Mi Nuong went out into the garden to hear the beautiful voice. She felt she could not live without it, even for a single day.

Autumn passed, and one afternoon the wind changed direction. The strange and beautiful voice could no longer float into the garden. Mi Nuong grew pale and weak, refusing to move from her bed. Her parents, not understanding what had happened to their daughter, became sick with worry. They called in dozens of famous doctors, who filled the castle storerooms with hundreds of expensive and rare medicines. One doctor tried a potion of ginseng. Another made a broth from the antlers of a young deer. Still another insisted that ground up tiger's bone would definitely supply the cure. But Mi Nuong only grew worse. For weeks, she lay in bed, thin as the silken sheets that covered her. Her parents became nearly hopeless with grief.

Finally, one of Mi Nuong's favorite handmaidens spoke up. Not being able to bear the sight of her mistress gradually dying, she told the mandarin and his wife about the strange man's beautiful voice. The stricken parents immediately ordered their soldiers to scour the countryside, seeking the singer with the golden voice in order to bring him back to the castle.

After searching dozens of tiny villages, a group of scouts arrived at the small hamlet just above the bend in the river. They inquired about the golden voice, and the villagers immediately told them about Truong Chi. When the soldiers arrived at his cottage, however, they found that he had gone fishing. For several hours, the soldiers waited. The villagers watched and worried about what was going to happen to Truong Chi. Some people thought he might have said something disrespectful of the mandarin, which would lead to a severe punishment. Some thought he had committed a rebellious crime. Others felt more hopeful, because Truong Chi was such a gentle man. In his entire life, he had never said an unkind word about anyone. Still, as the hours passed, the anxious villagers came up with every scenario they could imagine.

When Truong Chi finally returned to the village, he knew immediately that something strange had happened. Everyone was looking at him with sympathetic eyes but no one dared to tell him that the mandarin's soldiers were waiting for him. No one would speak because they were too afraid.

Truong Chi trudged back to his cottage and was shocked to see a dozen soldiers waiting for him. Without bothering to explain the reason for their mission, they told him that he'd been summoned to the mandarin's castle at once.

Upon arriving the castle, Truong Chi, wearing his ragged clothes and with his body still unwashed from a day of fishing, immediately found himself ushered into the mandarin's chamber. The mandarin took one look at the poor and ugly man and kicked him out of the room. A moment later, however, the mandarin's wife came in, tears in her eyes, saying that their precious daughter refused to eat or drink anything and, half-delirious, kept calling for the singer.

The mandarin was confused. He ordered his advisers to come to his chamber. "How can I let her see him?" He asked. "How can I let my beautiful daughter breathe the same air as this piece of filth?"

The advisers sat quietly for a long time, contemplating the difficulties of the situation. Finally, the chief butler, the most respected adviser of them all, spoke up. "I am only your stupid and foolish servant and although I have no right to even open my mouth, I must say that I believe the best solution will be for you to let her see this man."

"No, impossible!" the mandarin shouted, knocking his fist against the table. "How could I sully my precious possession in that way?"

Now, the chief butler was clever. Although he would never have said such a thing, he knew that he was much more clever than his master. He thought about the ugly face of the fisherman, and the poor man's ragged clothes. He thought about the beautiful mandarin's daughter and the life of luxury she had always known. "Lord," he whispered soothingly, "Let me assure you. Seeing his face will be the thing that cures her."

The mandarin still did not understand the clever reasoning of the butler, but he was desperate enough to try anything to save the life of his daughter. Heaving a great sigh, he raised a finger, signaling to his servants to lead Truong Chi back into the chamber.

When Mi Nuong learned that the singer of her dreams was coming to see her, she felt better in a minute. She was still very weak, but she managed to get up and have her maids help her put some jewelry on. The happiness and excitement turned Mi Nuong's pale cheeks a light pink.

When the maids brought Truong Chi into her room, Mi Nuong was startled. She had never seen, never even imagined, such a strange and ugly man, such sunburned skin, such ragged clothes. She gasped. Truong Chi gasped as well. For his part, he had never seen, never even imagined, such beauty, such a glow of light coming from another human being. Mi Nuong's image burned a permanent mark in Truong Chi's mind. The flame of love suddenly sparked in the heart of this young man who had never experienced anything like it before.

Mi Nuong's happy anticipation immediately turned to fear. She screamed and fainted. The maids hurried Truong Chi out.

Truong Chi had only seen Mi Nuong for the briefest moment, but the damage was done. Kicked out of the castle, he trudged back along the river bank to his tiny cottage and his rickety boat. In one instant, everything in his life had changed. He didn't want to do anything but reflect on the lovely image of Mi Nuong. Along with the intensity of his passion, however, came the knowledge that the beautiful girl would never love him back. This knowledge made him hopeless and desperately sad. After suffering a few weeks of this longing, Truong Chi couldn't bear it anymore. One afternoon, he stood on the river bank and began to sing. The whole village heard him, heard his deeply melancholy songs about love. He sang for hours, until the sun went down and a tiny sliver of moon appeared in the winter sky. Truong Chi sang until he couldn't sing another note and at that moment he collapsed onto the muddy bank of the river.

The next morning, the worried villagers came looking for Truong Chi. They found him lying motionless where he had fallen, looking very peaceful in death, with a smile on his lips, as if at the last moment of his life, the thought of Mi Nuong had cheered him. The villagers buried him right there on the river bank. Everybody cried. Even the animals and plants were full of tears. A few months later, a tree grew over Truong Chi's tomb. The tree was high and thin, but its branches were full of leaves. The villagers used the wood of this tree to carve beautiful and fragrant tea-cups.

As for Mi Nuong, the sight of ugly Truong Chi had made her healthy again, but she was no longer the happy, cheerful girl she had been as a child. She no longer felt love for the poor singer with the golden voice, but that space in her heart was now empty. She felt extremely sad, as if she had lost something very valuable in her life.

One day, one of her palace maidens offered Mi Nuong tea in a cup made of a strange kind of wood that was dark and very beautiful. Mi Nuong lifted the cup to her lips and, when she looked down into the liquid, she saw Truong Chi's image shimmering on the water. Suddenly tormented by regret, Mi Nuong began to cry. Her beautiful eyes filled with tears, which dropped one after another into the cup. The image of Truong Chi was shattered. For a moment, she heard it again, the sweet, melodious voice of the singer floating around her. Then it faded away, for the last time.

Princess Lieu Hanh, Tea-Seller of Ngang Mountain

തയതയതയതയതയതയതയതയതയതയതയതയ

I N Vietnam, people have long believed that life in Heaven is the same as life on Earth. They say that the inhabitants of Heaven have emotions and experiences just like ours. The happiness, sadness, anger, passion, love, hatred, sympathy, and jealousy that we experience on Earth can feel just as profound to the inhabitants of Heaven. Unlike us, people in Heaven never die, but their emotions can still get them into trouble.

Many centuries in the past, the King of Heaven had several dozen children. Among those children, Princess Number 13 caused the most trouble. Her name was Lieu Hanh, and she had such a strong personality that she had trouble following the rules of Heaven. She often started arguments with her sisters and brothers, insisting that they let her play with their toys. On two occasions, she rode her horse up the staircase. She often arrived at royal banquets wearing clothes that were torn and dirty, which very much embarrassed her father, the king. Over and over again, he tried to teach her to behave, but Lieu Hanh was very stubborn. She had a strong character and refused to change.

One day, Lieu Hanh got into an argument with three of her sisters when she insisted that they acknowledge that she was the most beautiful princess. Lieu Hanh's sisters were fun-loving and good-natured girls, and the silliness of Lieu Hanh's demand made them laugh. Their laughter enraged Lieu Hanh. In a fit of spite, she picked up a jade cup and threw it against a wall, causing it to shatter. Unfortunately, the jade cup had been her father's favorite. When he saw what she had done, he became furious and decided that only drastic measures would teach Lieu Hanh a lesson.

Calling his daughter into the grand throne room of the palace, the King of Heaven proclaimed, "No daughter of mine will behave this way. Today I banish you to Earth for 100 years. I don't want to see you again until you have learned to behave."

All the tears and begging from the queen and the other heavenly princesses could not convince the king to change his mind. Finally, Lieu Hanh, full of sadness and regret, said goodbye to her family and descended to Earth.

Lieu Hanh could have chosen any place on Earth to live, but she settled on a quiet clearing near the top of Ngang Mountain. The spot was peaceful enough to give her time to think about her life and her future, but not so desolate as to make her feel lonely. It lay on a road along which many travelers passed. Although Lieu Hanh was high-spirited and very stubborn, she also had a strong desire to help people. She decided to open a tea shop here to offer food and drink to weary travelers.

Ngang Mountain sits between the northern and southern halves of Vietnam. In those days, if you wanted to travel from one region to the other, you had to cross that mountain. The presence of so many merchants carrying valuable goods, however, attracted many thieves. Dozens of traders had been murdered, kidnapped, or robbed. Travelers had taken to moving in large groups, and they always hurried to cross the entire mountain between the hours of dawn and dusk. No one wanted to be caught on that mountain at night. People were in such a rush to cross that they never even stopped to rest.

When people heard that a beautiful young girl had opened a tea shop right in the middle of the Ngang Mountain pass, they could hardly believe it. Not only was Lieu Hanh the first woman to open a business on the mountain, no man had ever had the courage to do it, either. Where had she come from? they wanted to know. And, why wasn't she afraid?

Within a week of its opening, Lieu Hanh's tea shop had become very crowded. One reason was that travelers, in their rush to get over the mountain, were very thirsty by the time they reached the top. The main reason, however, was curiosity—one character trait that most human beings share. The news about Ngang Mountain's beautiful young tea seller spread very far and very fast. And along with this news passed a very interesting rumor: Travelers who only stopped to eat or drink would have no problems there. But anyone who tried to flirt with or harass the tea-seller would either go crazy or die. Within a month of Lieu Hanh's settling on Ngang Mountain, the place became very safe. No thieves dared to go near it anymore.

The news about the Ngang Mountain tea stall spread to the Royal Palace, where the king lived with his large family. Everyone in the palace found the story of the beautiful young tea seller to be very interesting, but no one's curiosity was greater than that of the king's eldest son, the crown prince. He was a proud and stupid young man who spent most of his days eating extravagant meals, drinking wine, and chasing women. When he heard about the girl on the Ngang Mountain, he wanted to go and see her himself. One day, when the king went off to visit the coastal areas, the crown prince organized a group of servants and soldiers to sneak away with him from the palace. Disguised as a group of rich merchants, they headed for Ngang Mountain.

Lieu Hanh knew that the crown prince would come to look for her, and she expected that his stupidity and pride would get him into trouble. Out of her sense of fairness, she decided to warn him. When the prince and his group stopped at the foot of the mountain to rest, Lieu Hanh turned herself into a peach tree. The tree was lovely to look at, perfectly formed, with branches covered in deep green leaves. But it had only one peach.

When the crown prince saw the solitary peach, he said, "Look, even though this tree only has one peach, it's big and looks so ripe. I want to taste it." He ordered a servant to climb the tree and pick the peach. The servant snapped the fruit off the branch, climbed down the tree, and presented it to the prince. Up close, the peach looked even more enticing, as if it were about to burst with ripeness.

As soon as the prince took the peach, however, something strange happened. It began to shrink. Within only a few seconds, it had completely disappeared. The servants, and even the soldiers, cried out in fright. "It's a sign," said the prince's most trusted servant. "Ghosts inhabit this tree. We must go back to the palace."

"Nonsense," the crown prince laughed. Facing the fears of his servants, he felt himself to be a very brave man, but his courage came from stupidity. He could not understand that the shrinking peach had been a warning from Lieu Hanh. Now he announced to the group, "Come on, you cowards. We'll continue our trip."

They arrived at the tea-shop very late in the afternoon.

The tea-seller's beauty went far beyond what the prince had imagined. He whispered to his trusted servant that she looked like a being from another world. Unable to take his eyes off Lieu Hanh, he ordered a twelve-course banquet for himself, a banquet that it took until well past sunset to finish.

After he had finished eating, the crown prince stood looking at the moon. "It's late already," he said to Lieu Hanh. "My group would like to stay here overnight. We'll leave tomorrow."

Lieu Hanh shook her head. "I live here alone. I don't want men to sleep here. A new village has just been built near here, so you can easily sleep there."

Lieu Hanh was giving the crown prince a second chance, but, again, he didn't see it. Instead, he insisted, "We won't do anything to bother you." He said that his group would set up their tents outside in the yard and that he himself would only need a small corner of her shop in which to hang his mosquito net. He promised that he and his men would do nothing to make Lieu Hanh unhappy.

Lieu Hanh shrugged her shoulders and turned away, saying, "Well, in that case, it's up to you."

Not noticing Lieu Hanh's anger, the crown prince ordered his servants to set up their tents outside and to arrange a special bed for him in a corner of the tea-shop.

That evening, after everybody else had gone to sleep, the crown prince stayed up very late, talking to the tea-seller. Lieu Hanh was very patient. She listened to a dozen stories about the crown prince's luxurious life, and she answered many stupid questions about her own life, too. As the night went on, the crown prince grew more and more forward with the young woman. He sat very close to her and whispered indecent things into her ear. After one particularly vulgar outburst, Lieu Hanh stood up and walked out of the room. The crown prince, drunk with lust for Lieu Hanh, lost all discretion and ran after her.

Lieu Hanh had only disappeared for an instant, but she had accomplished a lot. Catching a monkey at the edge of the forest, she turned it into a lovely young girl. She told the young girl to sit down on the bed, while she herself hid behind the door to watch. When the crown prince ran into the room, he didn't find Lieu Hanh, but this new girl seemed beautiful enough to satisfy him. Sitting next to her on the bed, he took her hand and kissed it. The girl smiled sweetly and did not fight back. But when the crown prince tried to pull her down onto the bed with him, she suddenly turned back into a monkey, bared her teeth, and bit him. The prince screamed and fainted.

The prince's servants and soldiers rushed in to save him. They found him lying unconscious on the floor. Lieu Hanh was nowhere to be seen. Not knowing what else to do, they made a special hammock and carried the crown prince back to the palace.

The queen and the palace concubines at first tried to hide the bad news from King Le. They secretly invited famous doctors from everywhere in the country to the palace. After many attempts, the doctors were able to wake the crown prince, but he could remember nothing at all about his former life. All day long he sat silently, staring at the wall. Whenever someone asked him something, he merely shook his head and smiled. The queen, knowing her son's ailment could be fatal, finally told the king.

King Le was despondent over the news of his son's illness. He summoned all of his advisers and asked for their advice. One mandarin suggested asking the Eight Diamond Generals from the Eastern Sea to cure the prince.

The king looked perplexed. "Who are these generals?" he asked.

The mandarin bowed his head very low and told the story. In ancient times, the female Buddha had dropped two enormous lotus flowers into the Eastern Sea. The flowers had remained fresh and fragrant for 800 years and then, one day, each lotus gave birth to four men. The female Buddha sent the men to eight different regions of the country, ordering them to fight against ghosts, devils, and monsters. Blessed with magical powers, these warriors could do almost anything to help people suffering from terrible problems. "Common people call them the Eight Diamond Generals," the mandarin explained.

The king sighed. His son's illness had made him realize his own deficiencies. Now he looked at the mandarins and, with deep sadness in his voice, he said, "I may be the king of this country, but there are so many things I need to learn. Please, help me. Our people are good and they deserve better lives."

The mandarins bowed. They admired the king for his modesty and love of his subjects, and they pitied him for the troubles he was suffering over his son. One of them said, "Your Majesty, the Eight Diamond Generals can surely help to cure the crown prince. But we must hurry. If his sickness lasts too long, it will be more difficult to cure."

King Le agreed. Using one of his mandarins as a chief emissary, he sent to the Eight Diamond Generals a delegation bearing many precious gifts. The Eight Diamond Generals received the delegation, but sent the presents back, along with a very powerful medicine to cure the prince. "We know King Le is a generous and benevolent king," they explained. "We will do whatever we can to help."

The crown prince took one sip of the medicine and

immediately recovered. Realizing that he had made a terrible mistake, he rushed to his father's side to beg for forgiveness. But King Le was very disappointed in his son. "You know how much I love you," he said. "But the mistake you committed is unforgivable. You lack responsibility, which is the most important quality of a leader."

With that, the king dismissed the young man as crown prince and bestowed the title on the second brother. Then, he added, "If you ever behave so badly again, I won't consider you my son anymore. Remember that!"

The prince hung his head and walked slowly out of the room. The king watched him walk away, then turned again to his mandarins. "Who is this woman Lieu Hanh?" he asked. "Why does she have such extraordinary powers?"

The mandarins went off to gather any information they could find, but when they returned all they could say was that she had killed many young men and made many others crazy.

The king, furious that someone would disobey the laws of the kingdom so blatantly, immediately sent his soldiers up to Ngang Mountain to bring back Lieu Hanh. But the more troops he sent, the more troops were defeated. Finally, the king turned again to the Eight Diamond Generals for help.

The battle between Lieu Hanh and the Eight Diamond Generals lasted seven days and seven nights. Neither side could win. The Eight Diamond Generals knew that Lieu Hanh had no fewer powers than they had and so they appealed to the female Buddha to give them something more. She gave them a magical bag. All they had to do was open the bag and all of Lieu Hanh's powers were drawn right into it. She had to surrender.

The Eight Diamond Generals carried Lieu Hanh to the royal palace and brought her to King Le. "Who are you?"

The king asked. "Who are your parents? How dare you break my country's law like this?"

Lieu Hanh looked the king directly in the eye and said, "My name is Lieu Hanh. My father is the King of Heaven. I made a mistake, and he punished me by sending me down to the Earth. You say that I have broken laws, but I have not. We all have a moral duty to punish men who harass young women."

Hearing Lieu Hanh's words, the king ordered his soldiers to release her. "You're right," he said, "as long as you never turn your powers on innocent people."

Lieu Hanh smiled. "I have been guilty of unfairness and spite in my life. Now I understand my duty to help and protect people. Please, have no fear of me in the future."

Princess Lieu Hanh said goodbye to the king and went back to Ngang Mountain, where she continued to live until the end of her hundred-year penance. Then, she flew back to Heaven.

The Vietnamese people have honored Princess Lieu Hanh by building a shrine to worship her on Ngang Mountain. People who need her help go there to pray to her and leave offerings. Everyone is careful not to touch anything in the shrine, however, because they know the force of Lieu Hanh's punishments.

THE INFANT GENERAL
OF PHU DONG VILLAGE

ΓΩΓΩΓΩΓΩΓΩΓΩΓΩΓΩΓΩΓΩΓΩΓΩΓΩΓΩΓΩΓΩΓΩ

LONG AGO, in a tiny village called Phu Dong, an old couple lived in a cottage at the edge of the rice fields. Both the old man and the old woman were hardworking, gentle people, and they lived in peaceful harmony with their neighbors. From the outside, their lives seemed complete, but no one in the village knew their sorrow. Sometimes, alone at night, they sat together and cried. The old man and the old woman wanted to have a child.

One morning, the wife woke up very early with a sudden desire to go out to the rice fields. Because her husband was still sleeping soundly, she tiptoed out of the house and went down the path toward the fields alone. From a distance, the fields looked normal. The young rice had grown as high as her waist, and its yellow-green color seemed to glow in the morning light. As she got closer, however, she came upon a puzzling sight. In the mud at the edge of the field was a giant foot-print, larger than any she had ever seen. Before running home to tell her husband, she put her foot into the foot print to measure it. At exactly that moment, she felt thrilled with a strange sensation.

A few weeks later, the old woman's belly began to grow. It wasn't long before she and her husband realized that she was pregnant. The couple waited anxiously for their coming child.

Nine months after the appearance of the huge footprint, the old woman gave birth to a handsome and healthy boy whom they named Giong. The new parents felt overjoyed with the birth of their son, but they quickly recognized that he was different from the other babies of the village. Most babies screamed with their initial gasp of air after birth. Giong never uttered a single sound, not even that first life-greeting cry.

Like flocks of birds soaring through the sky, three years passed. Giong neither cried nor laughed. He didn't develop in any other way, either. While other children learned to crawl and play, Giong remained a tiny baby. All day long, he lay in his crib, eating and sleeping, sleeping and eating. His parents felt distraught, but they consoled each other. "So what?" they asked. "He is our son. If we did not love him, who would?"

Every day, Giong's parents tried to love him even more.

For a while, the other villagers found this situation very strange. They'd seen fat babies and thin babies, babies who grew as fast as new rice and babies who lay weakly in their cribs, as if prepared to die. The villagers thought they'd seen every type of baby under the sun, but none of them had ever seen a baby who didn't grow at all. After a while, however, they got used to Giong. Babies have a way of pleasing grown-ups, and eventually the villagers came to love Giong as much as they loved any other village child.

The Viet people had enjoyed years of peace, but one day the An King from the North invaded the kingdom. The An soldiers raced through villages, sacking people's homes, raping women, burning houses, and murdering people for the sheer pleasure of it. The Viet people's leader, the Hung King, sent his armies out in defense, but the enemy were clever in battle and easily defeated the Viet troops. Soon, the very existence of the Viet nation lay in doubt. In desperation, the Hung King ordered his representatives to scour the countryside, looking for any talented people who might be able to help defend the kingdom.

A few days later, an ambassador arrived in Phu Dong's village square with the king's message. His announcement floated through the streets and into the room where Giong's mother was playing with her baby on the bed. Hearing the announcement, she smiled sadly. "My little son, you're so small. When will you be able to help the king save the country?" she asked.

At that moment, baby Giong sat up on the bed. "Mother," he said, "please invite the ambassador in to speak with me."

Giong had never sat up before, much less talked, and now his startled mother could only stare at him. When she failed to respond, his voice became more urgent. "Mother, please hurry," he said.

Finally, she collected herself enough to say, "My little son, the ambassador came on the king's business. I'm only a woman. How dare I interfere?"

"Mother, don't worry," said her son. "If you tell him about me, he will definitely come."

The old woman did not know what to do, so she called her husband and her neighbors in to help. They talked for a long time and, never having faced such a situation in their lives, they finally resolved to do as Giong asked. Just before the king's representative turned on his horse to ride away, the old woman ran out to the village square and meekly approached him. The official listened closely to her story and, finding it very puzzling, agreed to follow her home immediately.

In the bedroom, he found the tiny baby sitting up in bed. The king's representative had never treated an infant like an adult before, but, recognizing a wisdom and understanding in Giong's eyes, he asked, "Why do you request that I come here?"

Giong replied in a firm voice. "I have instructions for you," he said. "Go back to the palace and tell the king to make an iron suit of armor, an iron conical hat, an iron sword, and an iron horse. All of these things must be big enough for a giant to wear and use. Bring them here, and I'll help you defeat the enemy."

The king's representative decided at that moment that Heaven had sent Giong down to earth. Making a solemn bow, he hurried to his horse, then rode back to the palace as fast as he could, not even stopping to eat or sleep.

The Hung King heard this story with happiness and gratitude. Within minutes, he ordered the soldiers in the palace to use the iron in his ordnance depot to forge the armor, conical hat, sword, and horse that Giong required. Day and night, the soldiers hurried to finish their task. In three days, the armaments were prepared. They were so heavy that a 100 soldiers could not carry them. The 3,000 strongest men in the army had to do it.

Back in Phu Dong village, people were busy as well. At first, Giong's mother was very frightened. "My son," she said to the little child, "I hope you know what you're doing. Everybody's worried about the fate of the nation. When the soldiers bring you the armaments, what can you do with them?"

The baby tried to reassure his mother. "Don't worry," he said. "I can defeat the enemy. But you will have to feed me so I can gain strength."

The old woman cooked a meal of rice, pork, and vegetables for Giong. He finished it in only a few seconds. She cooked another meal, and then another, but as soon as she put the bowls on the table, he emptied them. The more she cooked, the more he ate, and the more he ate, the bigger he grew. Soon, he had eaten every grain of rice in the house. The old man and woman called their neighbors for help. The news quickly spread throughout the village, and soon people were arriving at Giong's house with huge pots of rice, platters of meat, and steaming bowls of vegetables. Even this enormous feast did not satisfy the growing child.

No one had ever seen anyone eat like Giong ate. Soon, the villagers had to race to neighboring villages and towns for help. The child continued to eat, only stopping long enough to say, "Mother, I need some clothes, too."

Everybody rushed back home, grabbed all the fabric they could find, and began sewing clothes. Giong was growing so fast, however, that by the time they finished making a piece of clothing, he had already outgrown it. It wasn't long before Giong had grown so tall that his head touched the roof, even though he was sitting on the floor. The neighbors in the village worked together. Then the people of all the villages in the region joined them, combining thousands and thousands of pieces of fabric into a giant suit of clothes. Not a single person refused to help. Everyone knew that if the enemy invaded their village, they'd lose more than property. They might even lose their lives.

The villagers were still trying to recover from the shock when the king's representative returned. The official bowed in front of the enormous boy and told him that the armaments were ready outside the house.

Giong squeezed through the door and stepped outside.

Standing in the fresh air, he lifted his shoulders and began to stretch. Within moments, he had become a giant, bigger than the biggest house and taller than the tallest tree in the village. In a booming voice that bounced off the mountains and flew through the forests, he shouted, "I'm a general sent by Heaven!"

Giong slid into the iron armor, put the conical hat on his head, picked up the sword, and bowed to say good-bye to his parents and the villagers before jumping on the iron horse. The horse came to life, leaping forward with flames shooting out of its mouth.

Giong galloped on the iron horse to the dark forest where the enemy were camping. The An King stood up to fight, but Giong's sword instantly sliced off his head. The horse galloped into the middle of the camp, and the flames from its mouth set a stand of bamboo on fire. Giong grabbed a handful of the bamboo and began to swing it. With each swing, he cut off a thousand enemy heads. The flames from the iron horse burned the enemy camp and raced across the entire forest. The enemy soldiers cried and screamed in terror. They ran in every direction, trying to escape. A few ran breathlessly back to their country, without looking back even once. Most, though, couldn't get away. At the edge of the forest, villagers and the Hung King's soldiers stood waiting. As soon as the enemy soldiers emerged from the forest, they were captured. Within only a few hours, the enemy was begging to surrender. The Viet country regained its peace and independence.

Giong's iron horse kept running. It ran all the way to Soc Mountain and galloped to the top. Giong took his armor and hat off and laid these on the ground. Then, the horse and its rider flew up to the sky.

Giong became a national hero. The Hung King, in remembrance of Giong's deed, named him *Phu Dong Thien Vuong*—Heaven's General from Phu Dong village—and the royal soldiers built a temple to worship him there.

Nowadays, a series of round ponds sits near the base of Soc Mountain. People say that these are the hoofprints of Giong's iron horse. Not far away, a village occupies the spot where the forest once burned, and people call it "Burned Village" in remembrance of the huge battle that took place there. Perhaps most strange of all, the bamboo trees in this area are not green but yellow, like the burning bamboo trees that Giong used as a weapon against the enemy. Villagers will tell you that yellow is not the bamboo's natural color, but the color it turned in the heat of the battle.

THREE DROPS OF BLOOD

ᴐᴈᴐᴈᴐᴈᴐᴈᴐᴈᴐᴈᴐᴈᴐᴈᴐᴈᴐᴈᴐᴈᴐᴈᴐᴈᴐᴈ

ONCE UPON a time in a small village, a young man and a young woman met and fell in love. They married and lived together in harmony, never fighting and never even raising their voices to each other. Everywhere they went, they went together. They worked very hard, and so, even though they were not rich, they always had plenty to eat and clothes to wear. Parents in the village often pointed them out to their children as a model for how young people should behave.

One day while they were plowing their fields, the wife became dizzy. She stood for a moment rubbing her brow, then collapsed to the ground. Her husband rushed over to her, then he and the other villagers carried her home. The village healer came to the house and tried to get her to drink a tea of traditional herbs, but the young woman never woke up. Two hours after collapsing in the field, she was dead.

The husband was inconsolable. He cried until he fell asleep, then woke and cried again. He cried until he lost his voice, until he was drained of tears, and blood flowed from his eyes. Nothing soothed him. He sat next to his wife's bed and refused to let anyone come near her. He wouldn't allow her body to be taken away. He sat next to her for three days.

On the third night, when the husband's exhausted family had fallen asleep, he remained awake by her bed. He stared at her face, feeling that his heart had broken completely. He could not understand why fate had been so cruel. He would never see her smile again, never hear her voice again, never feel her arms around him. With these thoughts in his mind, he threw himself into another fit of tears.

Suddenly, the window of the room opened. An old and gentle-looking man with silver-white hair and beard stepped inside. "Your love for your wife moves my heart deeply, but do not be so unhappy," he said. "Fate decides everything, and your fate will bring you happiness again in the future."

The husband, who had recognized immediately that the old man was a spirit from another world, knelt down before his visitor and said, "I can never be happy without my love. I beg you, please. Help me save her."

The old man turned and looked deeply into the dead woman's face. Then he shook his head and said, "I can see that she's not a faithful person. Do not be too miserable."

The husband burst into tears. "Oh, please," he sobbed. "I know that you can save her life. Please help me. I'll do whatever you want. Take my own life if it's necessary. But please save her. I won't be able to live without her."

The old man sighed and then, after a long pause, he said, "I'll help you. But remember what I said about her. You'll regret your decision in the future. Let me ask you one more time. Are you sure you want to do this?"

The husband was so happy to hear that his wife's life could be saved that he heard nothing else of what the old man said. "Of course! Of course!" he exclaimed, hardly able to contain his joy.

With a sad smile, the old man explained, "It's very easy to save her life. All you need to do is to poke one of your fingers and let three drops of blood fall into her mouth. Then she will wake up. But think twice before you do it." With that, the old man stepped back through the open window and disappeared.

The husband, worried that he may have only experienced a beautiful dream, hurried to follow the old man's instructions. He took a pin and pricked his finger, then gently opened his dead wife's mouth, and let three drops of blood fall onto her tongue. In a few seconds, her cheeks became pink. She blinked her eyes and smiled at him. When she saw the expression on his face, she asked, "Why are you so happy?"

When he told her what had happened, she began to cry. She reached up and touched her husband's cheek, then whispered, "Darling, you saved my life. It's yours now. I will love you and remain faithful to you as long as I live."

The husband's exclamations of joy woke their families and the neighbors. Soon, the whole village had gathered to hear the story. Everyone was shocked to hear about the old man and even more shocked to find that his instructions had been true. Before the sun came up on another day, the entire village had a celebration in honor of the miracle.

After that, the young couple's life went back to normal. Now, however, the husband refused to let his wife do hard work in the fields. He was too afraid that she would become exhausted again. Thus, when he went out to the fields in the morning, she stayed behind, taking care of the lighter work in the home.

The young woman soon grew tired of staying home alone all day. After she'd completed her housework, she would often walk through the village, looking at the shops and buying clothes and jewelry. No one in the village had failed to notice that, since coming back from death, she had become much more beautiful. In fact, she was now the most graceful woman in the area.

One day, when her husband was working in the field, the wife went to the river dock, where merchant ships harbored, to see if any of the ships carried anything she might like to buy. The night before, a ship had arrived that she had never seen before. It was beautifully decorated with ivory and rare wood, and she grew curious. An old man on the dock told her that the new ship traded in precious goods like silk, jade, and satin. Filled with excitement over the prospect of seeing such rare items, the young woman hurried down to have a look.

When she stepped on board, she was immediately startled. She had spent her life living in a small village, and she had never seen such luxury before. For a long time, she stood on the deck, captivated by the sight of huge reams of exquisite cloth, boxes full of fine jewelry, and baskets spilling over with sweet-smelling soaps and lotions. She knew that she must have looked silly just standing and staring at all the wonderful items, but she couldn't turn her eyes away.

The captain of the ship was startled as well. He had never seen a woman as beautiful as the one who now stood on the deck of his ship, captivated by the sight of all the precious objects. With a smile on his lips, he approached her and gallantly bowed. "Madam, I would like to express how deep an honor it is for me to have such a beauty on this ship."

The wife blushed at this praise and said, "You have so many lovely things. I'm afraid I can't afford to buy them, but I want to look at everything."

"Spend as much time here as you like," the captain responded. "Even if you don't buy anything, I'd like to offer you a small present to thank you for the honor of your visit."

With those words, the captain opened a small lacquer box, lifted out a diamond necklace, and offered it to the wife.

The wife hesitated for a moment. She knew that she should not accept such a gift, but the diamonds beckoned to her like the lights of a ship far out at sea. She lifted a single finger and touched it. Then she touched it again. Finally, she decided just to try it on for a moment before handing it back. When she saw her reflection in the mirror, however, she was surprised. She had always been confident in her beauty, but now, with the diamond necklace around her neck, she wondered if she was not merely the most beautiful woman in the village, but perhaps the most beautiful woman in the world. Letting the diamonds glisten in the sun, she turned to the captain and smiled.

"Shall I take you for a tour of my ship?" the captain asked.

The wife nodded. He pointed down a flight of stairs that led below the deck, and the wife nimbly stepped down them. Before following her, the captain made a subtle gesture to his sailors to cast off from the dock.

The tour of the ship lasted for hours. The captain opened every box and every basket. With the diamond necklace still around her neck, the wife ran her fingers through mounds of satin and silk. She sampled fine wine and exotic teas. She rubbed sweet perfumes into her hair and tasted delicacies that she had never even known existed. By the time she recognized how late it was, the ship had sailed very far from home.

The wife burst into tears. "I must go back," she cried. "My husband is waiting for me."

"But what about all these beautiful treasures?" the captain asked. "Don't you want to keep them?" If she agreed to stay with him and be his wife, he promised, he would give her more luxuries than she could possibly imagine.

The wife looked up at the captain through her tears. He seemed to be a generous man, and he promised more than her husband could ever hope to have. If she stayed with her husband, she thought, she could never have fine jewels or beautiful clothes, much less all the other precious goods that the captain offered. She took another look at herself in the mirror. A woman as beautiful as she was surely deserved a better life. She wiped her tears away and looked up at the captain. That night, she became his wife.

That same evening, the husband came home from the fields and heard that his wife had been taken away in a ship full of precious cargo. Without another thought, he borrowed a boat from a friend and rowed off down the river to chase the ship. For many hours he rowed without stopping, but never caught sight of the great trading ship. Finally, he stopped at a village on the shore and asked if anyone had seen it. The people he met took pity on this man with the desperate face. They gave him whatever information they had about the direction the ship had taken. But they knew very little.

One day, two days, three days, a week, then two weeks went by. The husband had not seen a single sign of the ship. At the beginning of the third week, he arrived at a large merchant harbor full of trading ships. He got out of his boat and asked if anyone had seen the ship with the precious cargo. An old sailor told him that the ship had sailed from the harbor a few hours before.

The husband ran back to his boat and set off again in the water. This time, the great ship was traveling at a very slow speed, and he caught up with it very quickly. Climbing up to the deck, he found the captain and his new wife sitting outside enjoying the leisurely hours of their honeymoon. The wife jumped up as soon as she saw him.

"Finally, I've found you my love," said the husband, but as soon as he reached out his arms to hold her, she pulled away from him and disappeared down the stairs of the ship.

The first mate was a kind man who felt sympathy for the husband's predicament. He stepped forward and took the husband by the arm. "It's useless, my friend," he said. "Go back to your village and find yourself another wife." The husband shook his head, refusing to leave until his wife left with him.

The captain pulled a silk bag from his pocket and poured a handful of gold coins into his hands. "Your wife married me voluntarily," he said, "but I offer you these coins as compensation."

The husband had never been so close to so much money in his life. If he accepted the coins, he would never have to work again. But he didn't even see them. He looked the captain in the eye and said, "Tell my wife to come out and meet me. If she is here voluntarily, let her tell me so herself. If what you say is true, I will leave immediately."

The captain was beginning to tire of this situation. He told his first mate to go downstairs and bring the wife back up. When she appeared, she looked down at the deck of the ship and spoke in a quiet but shameless voice. "Thank you for following me here, but I'm now the captain's wife. Please forget me and take the gold. You can use it to find yourself a new wife. Just don't bother us again."

The husband could not believe his ears. He looked at his wife very closely. She was dressed in a fine silk dress with strands of jade and diamonds around her neck. Her braided hair was wrapped in an intricate bun and many precious ornaments glistened within it. He had never seen her looking so beautiful before. She appeared so different from the wife he had known that he had to force himself to remember the plain clothes that she used to wear and the loving looks she had once given him.

"Darling, don't you remember those sweet days we had

together?" he asked. "We weren't rich, but we were never hungry or cold. No one could love you more than I do. And everyone in the village misses you. Please come home."

The wife looked up at him and burst out laughing. "Do you think I care about those poor villagers? You could sell every chair and table in that dirty village, and it wouldn't buy me even half of this necklace. You expect me to go back there and live with them again?"

The captain laughed as well, then he put his arms around her shoulders and said, "Be realistic, young man. She's mine now. Take the money and go!"

The husband ignored him and, turning to his wife, said in a firm voice, "Darling, I beg you for the last time. Please come home with me."

The wife shook her head. "Never. I say for the last time, take the money and go away."

"If that's what you choose, then I won't bother you anymore. Before I leave, I have one request. I don't want money. I want my three drops of blood back."

The captain was surprised. He turned to the wife. "What does he mean? Why would he want three drops of blood instead of money?"

The wife smiled and whispered, "He's stupid. He thinks that a memory would change my decision. But three drops of blood are nothing. Hand me a needle."

The captain was confused, but he called for a needle. The wife poked one of her fingers and started to count: "Here's your blood. One drop. Two. Three!"

As soon as she had spoken that final word, an expression of horror crossed her face. She grabbed her throat as if she couldn't breathe and collapsed to the deck of the ship. The captain and his crew rushed to help her but her heart had stopped beating. The captain looked up at the husband. "She's dead," he said.

Without another word, the husband climbed back into his boat and rowed away. The captain tried for a few minutes to resuscitate his wife, but her skin grew hard and cold as the last warmth of life drained out of her. He had no choice but to throw her body into the river.

The wife was soon forgotten. After all, the captain had only loved her for her beauty. A month later he met another beautiful woman and married her.

The husband returned to his village. He was depressed for a very long time and believed that he would never again trust a woman's love. But as time went by, his heart gradually healed, and he found himself in love again. His new wife was not as beautiful as the first, but she loved him with a full heart that had no limits.

After her death, the first wife's soul turned into a mosquito. She flew everywhere, biting people in hope of getting her blood back. People say that if a mosquito manages to drink three drops of blood two things will happen: The mosquito will turn into a woman, and the victim will become a mosquito forever.

THE TOAD IS THE UNCLE OF THE KING OF HEAVEN

ONE YEAR, it didn't rain for a long, long time. The grass turned brown and died. Trees stopped bearing fruit. Flowers shriveled before they had a chance to bloom. Every creature on Earth, including humans, fell sick from thirst. All across the parched land, animals lay by empty streams, too weak to move.

Toad, whom all the other animals considered the wisest creature in the forest, realized they might all die if nothing changed. He decided to travel to the Kingdom of Heaven to ask the king why it hadn't rained.

At that time, the distance between Heaven and Earth was not very far. In order to see the king, one only needed to climb a tall mountain and cross the swinging bridge that connected Earth to Heaven's Palace.

On the way, Toad met a crab. The crab asked, "Mr. Toad, where are you going?"

"I'm on my way to visit the King of Heaven," Toad said. "I want to ask him why he hasn't made it rain."

Crab opened and closed her claws in excitement. "I was

wondering that same thing myself, because I haven't been able to find water lately. Can I come with you?"

"Of course," answered Toad in a very eager voice. Then the two started on the road again.

After a while, Toad and Crab ran into Rooster, who asked where they were going. "We're on our way to visit the King of Heaven," Toad said. "We want to ask him why he hasn't made it rain."

Rooster stretched his long neck in excitement. "I was wondering that same thing myself, because I haven't been able to find any corn. Can I come with you?"

"Of course," answered Toad in a very eager voice. Then the three started on the road again.

Over the course of the journey, Toad met many other creatures. A tiger, a chili pepper, a pestle, a patch of green moss, and a flock of bees all wanted to know the purpose of the journey and asked to come along. They appointed Toad as their leader.

The group trekked up the mountain, crossed the swinging bridge, and arrived at the gate to Heaven's Palace. A big drum hung outside the gate. Toad told the pestle to beat it three times. One of the servants of the palace opened the door and looked outside.

"What do you want here?" she asked.

Toad stood as tall as his small legs could muster. "I'm Toad," he said. "My friends and I have come here from Earth to ask why the King of Heaven hasn't made it rain. Does he know that the Earth is very dry now and that all of us are going to die of thirst?"

When the servant returned with Toad's question, the King of Heaven grew angry. "This puny toad and his dirty friends dare to question me on such a matter? I'll teach them a lesson. They need to learn what happens when one dares to challenge a king."

The King of Heaven ordered the centipede to go out and bite the toad. The king did not know, however, that the rooster, the biggest enemy of the centipede, was among Toad's group. After one strong peck, the centipede was in the rooster's stomach.

The King of Heaven became even angrier now. He ordered the big buffalo to rush outside and fight. But the buffalo was no match for the tiger and within a very few seconds, the buffalo ran away bellowing, never to be seen again.

Now the king understood that Toad and his friends were very well prepared. He came up with a plan that he knew would dispose of Toad's group speedily. He ordered his maid to tell the visitors to return to Earth because it would rain the next day.

The delegation traveled back down to Earth and went to Toad's house to celebrate. Everyone was optimistic, except Toad, who told his friends. "I do not trust the king. He probably has some bad intention toward us. We should be safe and prepare ourselves."

Although the others didn't share Toad's doubts, they agreed to follow his plan. Toad told the moss to hide himself on the roof of the house, the pestle to stand behind the door, the pepper to stay in the kitchen, and the crab to wait in the water jar. He told the tiger and the bees to go to sleep early so that they could save all of their strength for the next day.

Then, Toad turned toward the rooster. "And you, Mr. Rooster, have the most important duty in our group. You cannot go to sleep tonight. Instead, you must hide in the tallest tree, open your eyes as wide as possible, and crow as soon as you see anyone. Understand?" The rooster nodded, feeling pleased to have a chance to show off his strong and beautiful voice. After dinner, everyone went to their posts and waited, hoping that Toad was wrong.

That night, just as Toad had predicted, the King of Heaven ordered the Thunder God to bring his famous hatchet down to earth and kill everyone in the group.

Just as the Thunder God hovered above the roof preparing to land, however, Rooster spotted him. "Ooh! ooh! ooh! oh!" Rooster crowed.

The Thunder God jumped in surprise, lost his balance, and slipped on the moss. He toppled over the side of the roof and fell on the ground in the front yard. His hatchet landed near the door. The Thunder God, whimpering in pain, limped toward the door. At that moment, the pestle seized her chance. She jumped out from behind the door and knocked the Thunder God hard on the head. It was so dark that the Thunder God didn't know what hit him. With his head spinning, he rushed into the closest room of the house, which was the kitchen. The little pepper was waiting. She aimed at the eyes of the Thunder God and attacked. Immediately, the Thunder God's eyes filled with tears. Blinded, he groped his way through the kitchen looking for water, but as soon as he thrust his hand into the jar, the crab grabbed his fingers and bit hard. The Thunder God screamed, raced out of the house, and flew back to the sky without looking back once. He left behind the hatchet that he had loved more than anything else in life.

The next morning, the promised rain did not arrive. Toad and his friends walked back up the mountain, back across the bridge, and knocked again on the door of Heaven's palace. This time, the King of Heaven was more than prepared. He ordered all of his soldiers out to kill the members of the delegation.

But Toad's group was ready. The bees, well-rested from the night before, flew into the faces of the soldiers and stung. The battlefield turned to chaos as the soldiers cried out in pain, covered their faces, and ran away. The slow ones became the victims of the tiger's sharp claws. Within a very few minutes, Toad's friends had completely defeated the soldiers of Heaven.

The victors marched directly into the palace. Frightened by the power of Toad and his friends, the King of Heaven surrendered. He summoned the Rain God and scolded him for not making it rain for such a long time. Because the king was still the king, the Rain God didn't dare say a word. He hurriedly went to make rain at once.

Toad turned to the king and said, "You've forgotten to make rain many times. The droughts on Earth make the plants and the creatures suffer. Are we going to have to come back here every time?"

The prospect of having Toad and his friends come back again was more than the king could bear. In the nicest tone he could muster, he said, "No need. Whenever you haven't had rain for a long time, just give a yell to remind me. I'll order the rain immediately."

Toad and his friends happily turned around, crossed back over the bridge, and started down the mountain. As they descended, they noticed drops of rain coming down from the sky. Trickles, then torrents began to rush through the rivers and streams. Lakes filled up. The land became greener. Trees bore fruit and flowers blossomed everywhere. The birds went back to singing, and all the creatures ran happily through the forest. Toad and his friends said goodbye to each other, promising to keep in touch. They were all content with what they had achieved.

Since that time, tradition has it that the sound of the toad will bring rain. Vietnamese peasants continue to use this knowledge as a way to forecast the weather in their everyday life. Consequently, the toad, like a trusted elder in the family, enjoys the respect of everyone, inspiring the popular saying, "the Toad is the uncle of the King of Heaven."

TWO CAKES FIT FOR A KING

⌒⌒⌒⌒⌒⌒⌒⌒⌒⌒⌒⌒⌒⌒⌒⌒⌒⌒⌒⌒⌒

L ONG, LONG AGO, Vietnam was a tiny country, much smaller than the one we see on the map today. Although its borders did not extend very far, it was a beautiful land. The sky above it shone clear and bright. The ocean that lapped its shores was gentle and generous. Life was safe, peaceful, and wealthy. For a long time, one dynasty ruled the land, a series of kings known as the Hung Kings.

The most powerful of the Hung Kings had many, many sons, all of whom went by the name of Lang, which means Prince. Of all these sons, the eighteenth, Lang Lieu, was the one whom the common people loved the very best. Lang Lieu was not like his brothers, who all loved to spend their days relaxing in the palace, playing games, wearing beautiful clothes, and eating delicious foods. While his brothers enjoyed their lives in the palace, Lang Lieu spent his days wandering through the countryside, watching people farm the land. When he was old enough, he asked his father to allow him to move out of the palace so that he could live a simple life, growing rice with the peasants in the countryside.

Lang Lieu lived a happy life in a small village not far from the king's palace. After a few years, he married a young girl, a peasant's daughter. Her name was Hoa, which means flower, and even though she did not come from noble blood, she was very beautiful, intelligent, and kind-hearted. Lang Lieu and Hoa were deeply in love. They were always together. If the villagers saw Hoa, they knew that Lang Lieu would be somewhere nearby. Their love and happiness were so deep and pure that even the birds in the trees felt envious.

One day, the king summoned Lang Lieu to the palace. Upon arrival, he was surprised to find that all of his brothers were there already. All the princes wondered what could be the reason for this sudden summons from their father. After everyone sat down in the royal meeting hall, the king walked in. The young men stood and bowed.

"My dear sons," the king said, motioning for them all to sit down. "Today, I have called you together for an important reason. As you can see by my graying whiskers, I'm growing old. The time has come for me to decide which of you will inherit the throne. One month from today will be my sixtieth birthday, and I've decided to hold a contest. Whichever one of you brings me the most meaningful, the newest, and the best food for my birthday will inherit the throne." With that, the king turned and went back into his private quarters.

Of course, the king's announcement immediately threw all the Langs into an uproar. The most meaningful? The newest? The best? Every Lang had a different idea of what the king might like, and within minutes they had all dashed out of the palace, racing off to find the dish that best fit their idea of the ideal food. Some of the Langs went off into the deepest forests. Some climbed high mountains. Some sailed out to the most dangerous part of the sea. A few even journeyed to neighboring countries in hopes of discovering a really exotic dish.

While his brothers raced far from the palace in every direction, Lang Lieu walked back to his village with a look of worry on his face. When Hoa greeted her husband, she saw his expression and asked, "My dear one, what makes you so concerned?"

Lang Lieu sat down in the shade of the old banyan tree and told his wife what had happened. "As you know," he told her, "I don't have any ambition for the throne. My greatest happiness lies in having a comfortable and serene life here with you. But next month is my father's sixtieth birthday. I want to do something to express my love for him, and I don't know what to do."

Hoa smiled and kissed her husband's cheek. "I'm sure you'll find something special," she said. They sat for a while in the shade of the tree and when the sun went down they went into their house to have dinner and rest.

Over the course of the next few weeks, Lang Lieu thought a lot. He didn't go wandering to faraway places searching for exotic delicacies because he knew that his father lacked none of those things. But what could make his father happy?

Almost a month passed and, with only two days left, Lang Lieu still had not decided what to bring to the king's birthday. Many of his brothers had already returned from their searches. They brought back baskets and trunks, boxes and bundles. They were so optimistic about their chances for success that they kept their selections secret out of fear that their gifts might be copied by someone else.

That afternoon, Lang Lieu sat on the edge of a rice paddy that had just been harvested a few days before. Harvest season was his favorite time of the year. The fields gave off the sweet smell of just-cut rice. Young children herded ducks across the paddy stubble, fattening the birds on the fallen grains of rice. The sounds of the children's voices, their laughter, and songs made Lang Lieu smile. But in his heart, he felt sad. Over the past few weeks, his face had grown pale from worry and thought.

Hoa was concerned that Lang Lieu might get sick. Now she filled a tray of food and carried it out to her husband in the field. "My darling, please eat something. Even if you're not hungry, eat to make me happy. I've cooked a simple meal, but it's something you love, new rice from the field. It's so fragrant and delicious, surely this will soothe you."

Lang Lieu stared down at the bowl of pure white rice. Its delicate aroma floated up into his nostrils, and, just as Hoa had predicted, the fragrance soothed him. Suddenly an idea came to him. "Why don't I try to make something from rice?" he asked. "What else could be more valuable to people's lives? We may eat ten, twenty, a hundred other dishes, but do any of those dishes really matter? No. Rice, only rice, is the food that sustains us."

With a bit more thought, Lang Lieu's new idea was complete. He turned to Hoa and said, "I'll make two new kinds of cake, both from rice. One will have a square shape and will symbolize the Earth, reminding us of the square plots of land from which we grow our crops. Inside the cake will be rice and salt, the two essential needs in people's lives, and green beans and pork to symbolize plants and all the creatures of the earth. I'll wrap that cake in *dong* leaves, giving it the dark green color of nature. The other cake will be white, perfectly white, and will have a round shape to symbolize the Sun, the master. I will make that cake from nothing but the purest rice."

Hoa giggled with delight. "I understand," she said, clapping her hands together. "The square cake will symbolize your mother, so kind and giving, holding every creature inside of her. And the round one will symbolize your father, noble and majestic, shining upon us all with his glorious light. Is that correct?"

Lang Lieu looked at Hoa admiringly. "In this life, no one could understand me better than you, my love," he whispered. Hoa was so happy she blushed, which made her even more beautiful.

The next morning, on the final day before the party, Lang Lieu and Hoa woke up very early. She washed the green banana leaves that they would use to wrap the cakes. He filled several baskets with the purest rice. Then they prepared the green beans and chose the best pig in their pen. The villagers came to help them kill the pig and prepare the cakes. Hoa used red and pink strings, the colors of luck and joy, to tightly tie the leaves around each one.

By that afternoon, everything was ready to be cooked. The young couple built a fire and put the cakes into the cooking pot to boil. If the fire were too high, it would overcook the cakes. If it were too low, the cakes would never cook through. Because of this delicate process, Lang Lieu and Hoa decided to stay up and look after the fire. All night long, they sat watching and tending to the flames. The rest of the village had gone to bed, and the two talked and talked, remembering the day they first met, the day they fell in love, and discussing their dreams for their future. The night was long, but neither Lang Lieu nor Hoa felt tired at all.

When dawn arrived, the cakes were cooked. They peeled the banana leaves off the round cakes, revealing bright white discs that seemed to glow like the morning sun. They left the square cakes in their dark green leaves, giving them the color of the fields and the forests. Lang Lieu arranged all of these cakes on a tray, half square, half round, half green, half white, the colors and shapes complementing each other perfectly.

That evening, the Hung King's palace was beautifully decorated with candles and flowers. The queen and the concubines wore their most beautiful dresses and their most expensive jewelry. All the princesses wore silk gowns and satin slippers. The palace musicians played one happy melody after another. In the next room, where the competition was to be held, trays of luscious foods filled every table. Not a delicacy in the world was missing. There was a platter of grilled bear's hands, a bowl of pureed tiger's livers, a cauldron of shark's fin soup, a dozen swallow's nests balanced on the branches of a golden tree, phoenix barbecued over a fire of mahogany logs, and a large and steaming salad made from the rarest blue-green sea-cucumber. Everything looked wonderful and smelled even better. The guests at the party were having trouble talking to each other because the food made their mouths water with hunger.

Only Lang Lieu's tray failed to cause any salivation. With all the fantastic delicacies filling the other tables, the simple platter of square and round cakes merely made the other Langs burst out laughing. Lang Lieu didn't mind. He sat quietly and waited.

At seven o'clock, a bell rang loudly. Everybody stopped talking and pulled their eyes away from the food. The Hung King, looking more regal than ever in his ceremonial yellow robes and wearing the golden crown on his head, stepped into the contest room, followed by his most important mandarins. He stood for a moment in the center of the room, gazing over the guests and the table full of food. Then he said quietly, "So, let the competition begin."

Over the course of the next hour, the king walked from

table to table, tasting every single dish. After each bite, he shook his head. "I've tried that before," he said, after swallowing a spoonful of shark's fin soup, "and I didn't like it the last time." He took a bite of barbecued phoenix and shrugged, "I tasted this dish last year on a diplomatic visit across the border." He tried the pureed tiger's liver and grimaced, "My own cook provides food more delicious than that."

Wherever the king walked, the faces of the Langs, full of happy anticipation, turned to disappointment. Finally, the king walked over to Lang Lieu's modest tray. He paused with surprise at the sight of the strange-looking cakes, then turned to ask his trusted mandarins, "Have you ever seen these dishes?" The mystified mandarins all shook their heads.

The king turned to Lang Lieu. "What kind of cakes are these?" he asked.

Lang Lieu knelt down in front of his father and quietly disclosed the ingredients and explained the meaning of each cake. Then he added, "Father, I think that in this life, there is nothing more essential than rice, and there is nothing more precious than parents' love for their children."

The king smiled. "Thank you for thinking of me and your mother. Have you named these cakes of yours, my son?"

Lang Lieu bowed his head. "I haven't thought of any name. Father, please help me."

The Hung King was very pleased. He looked around the room at all of his sons and said, "Of all of you, Lang Lieu is the only one who really thought of me and your mother. Love for parents is a very important quality for a king to have. I now declare that Lang Lieu will inherit my throne."

Everyone in the palace cheered. Even though some felt envious that Lang Lieu had inherited the throne, they also felt happy for their brother who had had the wisdom to find such a perfect dish. The birthday festivities began at that moment, and Vietnamese continue to remember the occasion as one of the biggest celebrations in the history of the country.

Lang Lieu and Hoa became the new king and queen. Under their reign, life became even happier than before.

Since that time, the square *chung* cake and the round *giay* cake have become the traditional Vietnamese foods that people make to offer to their ancestors on the Lunar New Year. Every year, people stay up all night, tending the fire, cooking cakes, chatting, singing, playing games, and, of course, telling the much-loved story of Lang Lieu and Hoa.

THE STORY OF WATERMELON ISLAND

CRCRCRCRCRCRCRCRCRCRCRCRCRCRCRCR

A LONG, LONG time ago, during the Hung Dynasty, a terrible storm swept across the ocean, sinking a trading ship that had been passing near the coast. A child washed ashore, and the king's subjects brought the little boy to the king, who decided to raise him as his own. This son, Mai An Tiem, was a very intelligent and talented boy. He quickly became the favorite of the king, who lavished attention on him and gave him many gifts. When Mai An Tiem grew up, the country's mandarins often came to him for advice, and appealed for his help whenever they asked for favors from the king. Some of the king's natural children became jealous.

When Mai An Tiem turned twenty, the king arranged for the young man to marry the third eldest princess, who was called Co Ba, or Miss Three. The couple moved into one of the king's most beautiful castles. Glistening treasures filled the rooms. Dozens of servants sat ready to cater to their every whim. Despite the richness of this life, Mai An Tiem remained a modest man. Every day, he ate simple, healthy meals of rice and vegetables, and only occasionally indulged in meat or fish. His clothes were solidly made but unadorned.

He spent his mornings overseeing the maintenance of the castle and his afternoons working alone in his garden.

Few people knew about this garden, but it was a magical place. Mai An Tiem tilled the moist black earth with such loving attention that tomatoes hung in enormous clusters on the vines. Forests of sunflowers grew as tall as trees. The carrots tasted so sweet that you could eat them for dessert.

One day, Mai An Tiem and Co Ba had a party. Orchids and roses filled the castle with such color and fragrance that visitors imagined an army of gardeners had produced them. The fruits and vegetables were so delicious that everyone talked about the beneficence of the king. Everyone competed to praise the wealth of the couple. Mai An Tiem only smiled and said, "Wealth doesn't matter."

Among the guests was Hau, one of the king's natural sons, a clever but lazy young prince who had been jealous of Mai An Tiem for a very long time. Hau's great dream was to make his adopted brother look bad in the eyes of the king. As soon as Mai An Tiem spoke, Hau recognized his opportunity. He excused himself from the party, rushed to the king's palace, and demanded an immediate audience with his father. "Mai An Tiem has spoken against you, my Royal Father," he declared. He repeated Mai An Tiem's exact words, then added, as embellishment, "And he said many other nasty things about our family."

Roaring in anger at the thought of such insolence, the king immediately sent a platoon of soldiers to Mai An Tiem's castle. The soldiers told the guests to go home, confiscated the beautiful treasures, and ordered the servants back to the palace. Within a very short time, Mai An Tiem and Co Ba stood in an empty castle. Only Co Ba's personal servant, Mo, and Mai An Tiem's personal servant, Man, remained, begging the soldiers to let them stay with the young couple. Because the king had given no order specifically banning servants, the soldiers relented.

As harsh as the punishment of having the castle stripped of its wealth may have been, it still didn't satisfy the king. He decided to banish the young couple as well, ordering his soldiers to take them to a deserted island in the Eastern Sea and leave them there with nothing but some clothes, a knife, and enough food to last them for a month. The king wanted to teach Mai An Tiem a lesson. He expected his son to beg for forgiveness, in which case the soldiers would return to rescue the castaways at the end of a month.

The young man did not satisfy his father's expectations, however. From the moment his possessions were confiscated until the minute he set foot on the island, he not only never begged for forgiveness, but he also didn't utter a single word. As the soldiers prepared to sail away from the island, they asked if Mai An Tiem or Co Ba had any message for the king.

With tears in her eyes, Co Ba nodded. "Please give our father our deepest wishes for a long and healthy life," she said.

Mai An Tiem picked up his wife's hand and squeezed it. Then he looked at the soldiers and said, "We thank our royal father for everything he has given us in the past, and we're sorry that he's angry with us now." He paused for a moment, then, in a quiet but firm voice, he said, "I still believe what I said about wealth. Two working hands can bring warmth and a full belly."

The soldiers returned to the palace. When they passed on the words of Co Ba, the king was so moved that he wondered if he had punished the young couple too severely. But when he heard what Mai An Tiem had said, his face grew hard. "If they want to scoff at my wealth, then leave them there," he said, adding, "From now on, we will behave as if those two never existed." From that day, he forbade the members of the court ever to mention the names of Mai An Tiem or Co Ba again.

Mai An Tiem, Co Ba, and the two servants now found themselves in a place that seemed very inhospitable indeed. They saw no houses, no boats, and not a single sign of human life. The waves lapped against a sandy beach, above which stretched a barren strip of land nearly bare of vegetation. Beyond that strip of land lay dense forest. In the distance, a range of hills climbed toward the sky. Co Ba, who, unlike Mai An Tiem and the two servants, had spent her entire life living in castles and palaces, now worried that they would starve to death in this place. Mai An Tiem tried to calm his wife. "Don't worry, darling," he said, stroking her head. "If we work hard, we'll survive."

Their first goal lay in finding shelter for the night. Setting forth from the beach, they began to explore, clearing a path through the forest toward the center of the island. The foliage grew denser, and they saw strange animals and trees full of fruits they had never seen before. After several hours, they came upon a shallow stream running from the direction of the hills. Although the water was rushing over rocks and fallen branches, it was so clear that one could see every pebble at the bottom of the stream. They stepped onto rocks that jutted out of the water and watched tiny multicolored fish hiding in the crevices of the rocks. On the other side of the stream lay the entrance to a cave.

"Let's use the cave as a shelter," Mai An Tiem proposed. "It will protect us from the sun and rain, and animals won't bother us there." The four lifted up their few belongings and picked their way across the stream.

Branches and dead leaves covered the floor of the cave, but it was also spacious and airy. Tired and hungry, they cleared a small area, then lit a fire and cooked some of the food that they had brought along with them. Darkness fell, and they took turns guarding the entrance to the cave. Despite the unfamiliarity of their surroundings, the night passed serenely, with nothing to scare them and only the sounds of the wind in the trees and the hooting of owls.

The next morning, they set off to explore the island. Not far from the cave, they found a large stand of bamboo. They immediately took out their one knife and began to make traps for hunting and nets for fishing. Later, they finished clearing out the cave. They collected mounds of dry leaves and used them to make soft cushions on which to sleep. In one corner of the cave, they set up a circle of large rocks as a spot for a fireplace, then they lit the fire and began to cook. By the time the sun set, a hearty meal lay ready for them.

Many days passed. Life became more stable. Every morning, one or two of them went out to hunt for food while the others wandered along the stream gathering fruits and nuts. At first, they worried that the strange fruits of the island might poison them, but when they saw rabbits or monkeys eating a fruit they decided it was edible. In that way, they introduced themselves to many delicious foods they had never even seen before.

In the evenings, the four sat around the fireplace, cooking and talking about what they had experienced that day. They preserved any meat they found and carved tools out of bones. They used threads of their tattered clothing to sew new garments out of animal skins. Co Ba's smooth hands had by now become callused with work. Mai An Tiem's white skin grew dark from the wind and sun. But their muscles were firm and their bodies were healthier than ever.

In this way, spring, summer, fall, and winter came one after another, then passed. A year went by. Then two. Then five. Mai An Tiem and his wife now considered their two servants closer to them than blood relations. The four were so used to life on the island that they rarely thought of the mainland any more. Co Ba gave birth to a handsome boy. Man and Mo married and afterwards had a baby girl. As the two families grew, they became even happier.

One day, after they'd been on the island for seven years, Mai An Tiem walked to the ocean to check his nets for fish. As he stepped out of the woods onto the barren strip of ground near the beach, he disturbed a flock of birds, causing them to fly away. Mai An Tiem noticed that the sandy ground where the birds had rested was scattered with shiny black seeds. He didn't know what kind of seeds they were, but he buried them anyway, hoping they would grow into something that he and his family could use.

Life was very busy for Mai An Tiem, and he completely forgot about the seeds. It wasn't until many months later, during one of the hottest days of the year, that he noticed a patch of strange plants growing in that spot. The plants grew close to the ground, and their thick vines stretched across the sandy dirt. Mai An Tiem squatted to look. Underneath the leaves, he saw an enormous fruit lying on the ground. Smooth and green with spots of white, it looked like a melon but was larger than any melon he had ever seen. He cut it in half and discovered a deep red pulp dotted with shiny black seeds. As soon as he opened the fruit, many birds dropped down from the trees and tried to eat it. Suddenly, Mai An Tiem recalled the day he had buried the seeds. If birds could eat this fruit, he reasoned, so could he. He dug his fingers into the pulp, scooped out a small piece, and tasted it. The fruit was sweet, fragrant, and full of juice. As he chewed and swallowed, he felt his mouth and throat and stomach grow cool. The heat of the day seemed less oppressive.

Mai An Tiem was so impressed that he cut a medium-sized fruit off the vine, hauled it onto his shoulder, and hurried home. When they tasted the melons, Co Ba, Man, and Mo immediately loved it. But none of the grown-ups were as happy as the children, who ate the sweet fruit until its juice ran in streams down their chins.

They named the fruit, which we know as watermelon in English, "Red Melon," in honor of its bright red hue. That afternoon, they gathered the seeds of the fruit to use to plant another crop. Soon enough, they were able to collect a second harvest. Now, Mai An Tiem had an idea. Taking a dozen or so of the finest melons, he carved his name and the location of the island into their rinds. Then he set them adrift on the ocean and waited.

The island was deserted, but it was not very far from a busy shipping lane. Before long, several merchant ships pulled the melons from the sea. The sailors also loved the delicious fruit, and, following the instructions on the rinds, they came to the island, hoping to find more of it. When they met Mai An Tiem's family, they proposed to buy the fruit. Mai An Tiem refused to take any money in trade, however. He lived on a deserted island. What good was money to him? In exchange for his melons, he asked for knives, fabric, salt, tea, and other goods that they had not been able to make for themselves on the island. The sailors readily agreed, and word of the fruit quickly spread among them. Many ships began to arrive and, by trading their melons, Mai An Tiem and his family acquired many of the goods that they had once had in their castle.

As news of the melons spread, people from the mainland came to the island to ask if they could take up residence and help with the planting and harvesting. The island's population began to grow and the island became famous for its special red melons.

It was only a matter of time, of course, before a servant presented the king with a piece of the bright red fruit. It tasted so good that the king wondered about its origin. When he heard the story about the far-away island, he thought of Mai An Tiem and Co Ba right away. So many years had passed that his anger had diminished. Now the king recognized the severity of his punishment. He ordered his soldiers to go to the island and bring his son and daughter home. When the couple arrived with their little boy, the king almost didn't recognize them. Mai An Tiem had grown into a powerful man. The once-delicate Co Ba was now a strong and healthy woman. The king felt happiness and regret at the same time, happiness at seeing his family again, and regret at what he had done to them. Now he recognized the truth in what Mai An Tiem had long ago said. Wealth really didn't matter. All the wealth in the kingdom could not have bought such strong bodies or healthy minds. No riches could purchase the happiness that shone in these young people's faces. At that moment, the king knew that Mai An Tiem had the wisdom necessary to be a great leader and so he named him heir to the throne.

Under Mai An Tiem's reign, the kingdom was peaceful and prosperous. The shipping industry became busier than ever.

Man and Mo stayed on the island and turned melon farming into a hugely successful enterprise. Traders came from near and far to buy the fruit.

Today, watermelon remains one of the favorite fruits of Vietnam. In summer, people eat it to cool themselves down. In winter, during the days of Tet, they set it on their altars as an offering to the ancestors. Some people believe that the color of a Tet watermelon's juice tells the fortune of the coming year. If the liquid runs clear, it's a bad omen, but if it's a deep, dark red, they will count on good luck.

THE STORY OF THACH SANH

IN VIETNAM, even the smallest villages have rich people and poor people. A rich family might have two water buffalo, a vegetable garden behind the house, and even several pigs. In the city, such possessions wouldn't make you rich at all, but in the village, two water buffalo, a vegetable garden, and several pigs could mean you're the richest family around. Poor, on the other hand, is just poor. Wherever you live, poverty means a hard life.

Thach Sanh's family was the poorest family in the village. The boy lived with his mother and father in a tiny hut near the spot where the other villagers threw their trash. Every morning, they woke to the smell of vegetables rotting in the dump. Every night, they fell asleep to the sound of rats digging through the piles of trash, searching for something to eat. The family worked hard, but their situation never improved. They slept on the floor, and they never had enough money to buy even the cheapest pieces of meat. They only owned one valuable thing, an ax that Thach Sanh's father used to cut wood.

When Thach Sanh was fifteen, life got worse. His mother came back from the market one day with a cough. Soon, she grew so sick that she could do nothing but lie on the floor and moan. Neither Thach Sanh nor his father was willing to leave her alone, so they took turns taking care of her. While three members of the family had once been able to work, now they were down to only one.

One evening, after they'd eaten only rice with warm water for dinner, Thach Sanh asked his father if they should sell the ax. His father shook his head. "Keep that ax with you, my son," he said. "No matter what happens, that ax will help you in your life."

That night, Thach Sanh's mother died. The father, overwhelmed with grief, passed away soon after. Now, Thach Sanh was an orphan.

The boy wanted to honor his parents in a way that they had never been honored in life, so he sold the hut and nearly everything in it in order to pay for a respectable funeral for his mother and father. After the funeral, he only had one possession left. Luckily, that ax was very sharp.

Thach Sanh went to live under a banyan tree at the edge of the village. The banyan was a thousand years old and so big that neither sunlight nor rain could penetrate its leaves. Thach Sanh liked living there. Even though he had to sleep outside, the air was fresh, and he didn't have to smell the stink from the dump. Every day, he took his ax into the forest to cut wood, which he traded with other villagers for rice and supplies.

Thach Sanh soon became the most sought-after woodcutter in the village. He had two things no other woodcutter had. One was the ax, which was so sharp it could cut through even huge logs very smoothly. Thach Sanh's other advantage was unusual strength. He carried loads of wood four times heavier than an average person could carry, and he still walked so fast that it looked as though he had nothing weighing down his shoulders at all.

Thach Sanh didn't think his life was too bad. He had more food to eat than he'd ever had, but he also experienced loneliness worse than he'd thought possible. At night, he lay beside the huge roots of the banyan tree and tried to pretend that those hulking forms were his mother and father.

One day, while Thach Sanh was off in the forest, a rice wine dealer from a neighboring village stopped to rest under the banyan tree. The dealer, whose name was Ly Thong, sat drinking rice wine for much of the afternoon. At dusk, he watched a teenage boy approach, carrying two huge loads of firewood. A thought suddenly came to Ly Thong's mind. "This kid is very strong," he told himself. "He could be very useful for my business." When Thach Sanh reached the tree, Ly Thong introduced himself very politely. Thach Sanh sat down next to him and they began to talk.

After some minutes of friendly conversation, Ly Thong made a proposition. "My family has only my mother and me in it," he said. "You're all alone here. Why don't you come and live with us? You can be my blood brother. My mother can be your mother, too."

Thach Sanh was pleased. Ly Thong was six years older and could advise and teach the teenage boy. From that moment, Thach Sanh began to call Ly Thong "older brother," and he began to think of him that way. Letting the blue sky be their witness, they promised to be brothers until the end of their lives. Then Thach Sanh followed Ly Thong home.

The lives of Ly Thong and his mother became much easier after the new brother arrived. Thach Sanh did all the housework and cooking, so neither of them ever had to do a thing. He also helped Ly Thong haul the rice wine and, because of Thach Sanh's unusual strength, Ly Thong could buy five times more wine than before. Money poured into his pocket as quickly as wine fills cups on a festival day.

A few years passed. One winter, a fire-breathing snake came to live near Ly Thong's village. No one knew where he came from. He destroyed rice fields and ate many people. The king offered a big reward to anyone able to kill the snake, but of the many young men who went off to try, none ever came home. Finally, people in the area held a meeting about the problem. They agreed that each month they would offer the snake one person to eat. The snake, who was lazy and tired of going out to find food by itself, accepted this deal. After that, the families took turns sacrificing their loved ones to the devil. A deathly atmosphere covered the whole area.

When Ly Thong's turn came around, he faced a real crisis. If he let Thach Sanh die at the hands of the snake, the rice wine business would begin to decline. But Ly Thong had no other choice. Who else but Thach Sanh was fit to die?

That evening, Ly Thong said to Thach Sanh, "My brother, tonight is my turn to guard the communal temple. I'm so tired. Could you please help me for one night?"

Without a moment of hesitation, Thach Sanh agreed. He picked up his ax and headed for the temple.

That night, while Thach Sanh was sleeping, the wind began to blow and a terrible smell woke him. He jumped up and, holding the ax firmly in his hand, rushed outside just as the snake, following its habit, rushed in. Thach Sanh raised his ax and whacked the snake in the middle of its head. Luckily, the forehead was the one vulnerable place on the snake's body, and the monster fell over and instantly died. Thach Sanh sat next to the body for the rest of the night. He had never killed anything before. He knew the snake was a monster, but still he felt terrible. At dawn, he slowly walked home.

When Ly Thong and his mother heard Thach Sanh's knock on the door, they were terrified. Surely, Thach Sanh's ghost had come back to punish them.

Ly Thong stood by the closed door and said in a trembling voice, "Please forgive me, my brother. I will worship you on this anniversary of your death every year of my life."

Thach Sanh laughed, and called through the door, "It's just me, Thach Sanh. I killed the snake. The body is out in the temple."

"Please don't lie to me. How did you kill it?"

"I just did. If you don't believe me, go see for yourself."

Ly Thong, still suspicious, opened the door slightly. As soon as he saw Thach Sanh's healthy face, he knew that the young man was indeed still alive. Suddenly, Ly Thong had an idea. Letting a look of horror cross his face, he said, "This is terrible. Didn't you know that the snake belonged to the king? You've killed it. The king is going to punish you."

Thach Sanh was frightened. "What should I do, brother?" he asked.

"Well, it was an accident," Ly Thong replied. "I'll do what I can to help you. Hide yourself somewhere, and I'll go beg the king's forgiveness. Don't show up here again. I'll come find you and let you know what happened."

Thach Sanh did not doubt a word that Ly Thong said. Saying goodbye to his blood brother and his mother, he put the ax over his shoulder and went back to the banyan tree where he used to live.

As soon as Thach Sanh disappeared down the road, Ly Thong hurried to the temple, cut off the snake's head, and took it to the king's palace to receive his reward. The king was so pleased that he gave Ly Thong a high position in the court, as well as bags full of gold and jade. Ly Thong and his mother settled into a very comfortable life in the palace.

That year, the king's only daughter reached marriage age. Many high-ranking young men proposed to her, but the princess turned them all down. The king, who was anxious to find a groom for his daughter, came up with a plan. Finding a fortuitous day on the moon calendar, he invited every prince from the neighboring kingdoms, every young mandarin, and every old mandarin's son to a festival. At the festival, the princess would throw the royal sphere into the crowd. The man who caught it would become the prince consort.

Rumors about the princess's beauty and gentleness spread across the land. When the festival day arrived, thousands of young men crowded around the palace hoping that fate would smile on them. Ly Thong stood among those men.

That morning, the sky was blue and cloudless. Sunshine warmed the earth and a breeze blew gently through the trees. Birds were singing cheerfully and flowers that had only budded yesterday were now in full bloom. The young men, dressed in their best clothes, whispered to each other that spring had finally arrived. Standing below the princess's balcony, each one secretly hoped that this beautiful day would be a good omen for him.

At precisely nine o'clock, the princess, in a magnificent long white gown, stepped out onto the balcony. Her beauty far surpassed what the young men had imagined, and now their young hearts beat even faster. A sweet smile appeared on her pink lips, which were as fresh as rose petals in the morning dew. When she spoke, her voice reminded all the men of the sound of a nightingale singing.

"Today I follow my royal father's advice," she said, turning for a moment to smile at the king, who had walked onto the balcony behind her. "I will throw the royal sphere. I want to thank you for coming to the festival, despite the time and distance. Later, after I have found my husband, my father will invite all of you to stay and join the wedding celebration."

When the princess finished speaking, two maidens stepped onto the balcony, carrying a golden tray. On it sat the five-colored sphere, which was covered in fine velvet and embroidered with the royal symbols of the kingdom. The princess gently rolled up her sleeves, displaying a small white hand and long, smooth fingers. She carefully picked up the sphere. Down below, thousands of men were absolutely silent.

Suddenly, a gust of cold wind swept across the palace courtyard and up to the balcony. Not a single cloud appeared, but the sky turned as dark as it would in a thunderstorm. At that moment, a giant eagle landed on the balcony, grabbed the princess, and flew away. By the time everyone realized what had happened, the eagle and the princess had disappeared. Up on the balcony, the king stood stunned. The two maidens were crying.

Finally, with his eyes full of tears, the king began to speak. "I thought today would be a happy day at the palace. Considering this change in circumstances, I hereby change the rules. Among all of you young men, whoever can rescue my daughter and bring her back to me can marry her. I don't care if you are rich or poor, from a noble family or not, just bring my daughter back alive."

Ly Thong, standing in the crowd in the courtyard, suddenly remembered his blood brother. He had not given a thought to Thach Sanh in months, but the young man was a great fighter. Who better to help Ly Thong find the eagle and win the princess?

Ly Thong rushed back to the old banyan tree. Thach Sanh was kneeling over a small pack, as if preparing to go somewhere. As soon as he saw his blood brother, he exclaimed with joy, "My dear brother, you've come just in time. If you'd come a moment later, you would not have found me here. How's our mother?"

"Mother's fine. She misses you terribly," Ly Thong said. "Where are you going?"

"I just saw the strangest sight," Thach Sanh said. "A giant eagle flew by, carrying a girl. I grabbed my slingshot, aimed at its neck, and shot. Unfortunately, I didn't have time to get a better shot. The stone only hit the bird's wing. It began to bleed, though, and I believe that if I follow the trail of blood, I can find the eagle's nest and rescue the girl."

This was good news for Ly Thong. "Why don't I go with you and give you a hand?" he asked.

Thach Sanh smiled and said, "I'd be so happy to spend some time with you."

The two men followed the trail of blood drops into a very deep forest. The canopy of trees became so dense that down on the ground it seemed almost as dark as night. Thach Sanh led the way, keeping his eyes on the drops of blood. Ly Thong, unwilling to be alone in this forest, hurried to keep up. After a long time, Thach Sanh came to a halt at the edge of an empty well. The drops of blood had disappeared.

Thach Sanh said, "Maybe the eagle's nest is at the bottom of this well. We'll have to go down there to get him."

Ly Thong leaned over and looked into the well. It seemed bottomless. He was not going to go down that well.

"Here's an idea," he said. "Let's make a long, strong rope, tie it to the edge of the well, and you can climb down there on it. I'll stay here and make sure no animal drags the rope away. If you see the girl, tie the rope around her waist and jerk it twice. I'll pull her up first, and then drop the rope down again to pull you up. What do you think?"

Thach Sanh agreed. Then the two blood brothers went to

look for rattan vine to weave into a long and sturdy rope for Thach Sanh to climb down.

After reaching the bottom, Thach Sanh hesitated for a few minutes, surveying his surroundings with the small candle he carried with him. This place wasn't just an old well, but a huge cave with many dark passages. From somewhere off to the right came the sound of someone weeping. "Who is that?" Thach Sanh asked. "Please let me know where you are so I can help you."

"Look down the narrow passage behind the large rock. I'm here," said the voice.

Following the instructions, Thach Sanh came to a small room with iron bars in front of it. Sitting inside was the young woman whom the eagle had been carrying that morning. Now, even in the dim candlelight, he saw how beautiful she was.

"Who are you?" he asked. "Why are you here?"

"I'm the princess," she said, explaining how the giant bird had kidnapped her. "The eagle wants me for his wife, and he would have married me immediately. Luckily, on the way back to this cave, someone shot him. Now he's gone to look for medicine. Who are you? How did you get here?"

"My name is Thach Sanh. I'm the one who shot the eagle. I followed the trail of his blood to rescue you."

The princess looked up at Thach Sanh with her lovely eyes. "You are very kind, but I don't think that's possible," she said sadly. "The eagle is strong, and you're all alone. We won't be able to escape."

Thach Sanh smiled and said, "Please don't worry. With my ax, I can easily kill him. If you step out of the way, I'll get you out of this room."

Thach Sanh chopped through the iron bars between him and the princess. Just as she stepped out of the room, the eagle returned. The sight of a stranger in his territory infuriated the bird. He charged straight for his young enemy. Thach Sanh raised his ax, ready for the attack. The princess, hiding in a corner of the cave, prayed for him.

Thach Sanh and the eagle fought for so long that the air grew heavy with feathers and dust. The eagle tried to pierce Thach Sanh's eyes with its beak, and its knife-like claws ripped at the young man's skin. Gradually, however, the giant bird grew weaker. Blood poured from ax wounds all over its body. Thach Sanh felt himself becoming stronger as he fought. Finally, the eagle collapsed from exhaustion. Within seconds, it was dead.

The princess ran over to Thach Sanh, then gasped when she saw a deep gash in the young man's shoulder. She made Thach Sanh sit down. Then, she tore off a sleeve from her gown and gently wiped and dressed the wound. Thach Sanh had not been treated so kindly since his parents' deaths and the gesture left him speechless. He became dreamy, breathing in the sweet fragrance of the princess's clothes. He forgot where he was. The world seemed very small just then, as if only the two of them lived in it.

The princess, too, felt moved. For the first time in her life, she stood so close to a young man that she could feel his breath send a soft breeze through her hair. As she touched his shoulder, her heart beat fiercely against her chest. Neither of them said a word. When she finished wrapping the bandage, he stood up. For a long time, the two of them stood looking at each other in silence.

The candle flickered. Thach Sanh suddenly remembered Ly Thong, waiting for them up above.

"We should go up," he told the princess. "My blood brother is waiting for us."

They walked to the rattan rope and Thach Sanh wrapped

it several times around the princess's waist. "Can't we go up together?" she asked.

Thach Sanh shook his head. "The weight would be too heavy. The rope could break."

As if she believed something bad would happen, the princess pulled a ring off one of her fingers. "My mother gave me this ring when I was a child," she said, handing it to Thach Sanh. "I've never taken it off before. Keep it with you. If anything ever separates us, take it to the palace and look for me."

Thach Sanh carefully placed the ring in the pocket of his shirt. "Don't worry," he said. "In a few minutes, we'll see each other again."

Thach Sanh gave two jerks to the rope. Ly Thong pulled the princess up. Then, as Thach Sanh waited for the rope to fall back down, Ly Thong hurled huge rocks down into the hole, blocking the exit.

The princess, screaming, watched in horror. All the emotion of the day swept over her and she fell unconscious to the ground.

As soon as the rocks started dropping, Thach Sanh rushed into a small passage to get out of the way. Watching the rain of rocks, he saw for the first time the treachery of his blood brother. A wave of sadness swept over him.

For a long time, Thach Sanh stood desolate, thinking about Ly Thong. He felt drained of energy and began to question his desire to live. When his thoughts returned to the events of the day, however, the memory of the princess reignited the warm flame in his heart.

"At least she's safe," he told himself. The thought of her gave him the urge to escape.

Thach Sanh searched up and down the cave. When the candle went out, he closed his eyes and, using his hands as a guide, moved along the passages, never knowing if he was nearing an exit or leading himself deeper and deeper into the pit. Room after room sat behind iron bars. Room after room contained human bones. Thach Sanh shivered at the thought of how many of the eagle's victims had died here.

After many hours, Thach Sanh heard a weak moaning coming from a back corner of one of the rooms. He cut through the iron bars and found a young man lying on the floor. Thach Sanh helped him sit up, then fed him some of the water and food he had in his pack. The young man slowly regained enough energy to explain that he was the son of the Emperor of the Ocean. "A week ago, I traveled onto dry land to explore," he whispered. "The eagle grabbed me and carried me back to this cave. I've had neither food nor water. I've grown so weak that I prayed I'd die. You have no idea how grateful I am for your rescue."

"I haven't rescued you," Thach Sanh said. "The way back out is blocked. We could both very easily die here."

The Prince of the Ocean squeezed Thach Sanh's hand. "We won't die. I know how to get out. I couldn't do it because the iron bars trapped me. Down this passage is a door to the sea. Every time the eagle used it, I could smell the ocean air."

Thach Sanh helped his new friend stand up and together they made their way to the end of the long, narrow passage, where a huge boulder blocked their way. Here, they felt cool air and saw a dazzling light seeping through cracks at the edge of the rock. When Thach Sanh pressed his face against the cracks, he saw blue sky and fluttering leaves. He took a deep breath, spread his arms around the boulder, and with all his strength he tried to push it out of the way.

At first, the enormous rock didn't budge. Slowly, however, it slid one inch, then another, then another, little by little easing open. Thach Sanh kept pushing and pulling until, finally, he created a gap big enough for himself and the prince to slide through. When they emerged from the cave, they fell to the ground exhausted, then slept through the rest of that day and night.

The sound of birds woke Thach Sanh. For a long time, he continued to lie on the ground, admiring the beautiful forest morning. Then, remembering what had happened, he woke the prince, who was still sleeping beside him.

"Please come with me to my kingdom," said the Prince of the Ocean. "My father will want to thank you."

Thach Sanh shook his head. "I don't need thanks, because you would have done the same for me. Anyway, how could I survive underwater?"

"Please," said the Ocean Prince. "I can help you. You saved my life, and I will consider you a friend forever." Although Thach Sanh had become suspicious of such vows, something told him that the prince was an honest man. After a few more minutes, he agreed to go.

The prince clapped his hand three times. The waves split into two parts, revealing a path just like a path on land. The prince led Thach Sanh by the hand and, as they walked, the waves closed up again behind them.

The Emperor of the Ocean was elated to see his beloved son. For a whole week, everyone in the ocean kingdom had frantically searched for him, but he had disappeared without a trace. Now, the king ordered his subjects to prepare a great celebration in honor of Thach Sanh. The prince took his friend to many regions of the ocean. They visited gardens with all kinds of rare plants and water flowers. Beautiful mermaids wearing vibrant-colored algae clothes thanked Thach Sanh for saving their brother, the prince. The whole kingdom, so happy with the return of the prince, begged Thach Sanh to stay with them forever.

After three days, however, Thach Sanh was ready to leave.

As spectacular as the ocean was, he missed the land, and he couldn't forget the lovely image of the princess.

The Ocean Prince wanted to have one last party for Thach Sanh. "At the party," he told his new friend, "my father will offer you many precious things. Don't take any of them. Instead, ask him for the old rice pot and the lute that he keeps in his storage room. Those two things will help you more than any gold or jewels."

Thach Sanh followed the prince's advice. When the Emperor of the Ocean insisted that he take some gift from the sea, Thach Sanh asked for the lute and the rice pot. Without a moment's hesitation, the emperor ordered his servants to go and get them. "You've made a wise choice," the king said. "Those two things are among my most precious possessions, but my son's life is the most precious of all. We would have liked you to stay with us forever, eventually sharing the water kingdom with my son."

Thach Sanh lowered his head. He was beginning to understand what true generosity and love could be, and the knowledge filled him with emotion. When he could finally speak, he thanked the king and the prince for all that they had given him and for all that they had taught him.

The prince led Thach Sanh back to the land. Just before saying goodbye, he told Thach Sanh, "You're very kind. Heaven will bless you for that. If you ever want to return here, just clap your hand three times, and I will send someone to welcome you."

Thach Sanh agreed. Then, carrying the lute, the rice pot, and the ax on his shoulders, he started off on the road to the palace.

Much had happened in the time since Ly Thong dropped the rocks down the mouth of the well. As soon as he was sure that Thach Sanh was dead, he carried the unconscious princess back to the palace. The king, so relieved to have his daughter home safely, was ready to let Ly Thong marry her immediately. Only one impediment remained. When she finally regained consciousness, the princess couldn't speak at all. Not only had her beautiful voice left her, but she didn't seem to remember anything, including her fiancé, Ly Thong. The king postponed the wedding and put Ly Thong in charge of finding a doctor to cure her. All the famous doctors in the land came to the palace to try to help the princess, but none of them could do a thing. All day long, she sat in the palace gardens, weeping.

When Thach Sanh arrived, he learned that the princess was sick. Taking the ring from his pocket, he gave it to the mandarin in charge of visitors and said, "Please give this ring to the princess and tell her Thach Sanh would like to try to help her."

The mandarin could see by its crest that the ring came from royalty. He told Thach Sanh to wait and hurriedly carried the ring toward the princess. Before the mandarin reached the garden, however Ly Thong stopped him and asked him when the next doctor was due to arrive. When the mandarin told the story, Ly Thong broke into a sweat.

"That man stole the ring," he said, and ordered Thach Sanh imprisoned immediately without any food.

Ly Thong knew nothing about the magic rice pot. Although the palace prison was dark and desolate, Thach Sanh hardly suffered. Whenever he felt hungry, he only had to tap on the iron lid of the pot and mounds of fragrant rice would appear in front of him.

Now that he was so close to the princess, Thach Sanh's longing to see her grew even worse. That night, while the whole country slept, he sat in his prison cell overcome with sadness. Finally, in hopes of consoling himself for a few minutes, he took out the lute and began to play a melancholy tune.

Thach Sanh remained a prisoner, but the notes of his lute escaped. They floated through the prison's gates, over the walls of the palace, and into the princess's room. Her eyes opened as soon as she heard the sound of the lute, that sorrowful song of a person mourning his fate.

The princess got out of bed, walked to her father's room, and said to him in a clear voice. "Father, please bring that musician here to me."

So glad to hear his daughter speak again, the king immediately ordered his servants to do as she asked. The palace guards led Thach Sanh up to the princess's room and as soon as she saw him she burst into tears and told her father the whole story. Thach Sanh then showed the king the bandage made from the princess's gown, which he had kept like a treasure in his pocket. The soft piece of fabric perfectly matched the missing sleeve on the dress the princess had worn on that unlucky day.

Now that he knew the true story, the king immediately ordered Ly Thong's head to be cut off.

"No," said Thach Sanh. "I cannot live with the knowledge that a man has died because of me. Please spare him."

The king accepted Thach Sanh's request. Instead of chopping off Ly Thong's head, he withdrew his royal ranking, stripped him of his groom's clothes, and ordered the soldiers to kick him out of the palace. Ly Thong crept back to his village. News travels faster than a ruined man, and by the time he reached home, a mob of people were gathered there to scorn him.

Thach Sanh married the princess that afternoon, and the

country celebrated for three days. Everybody in the kingdom approved of Thach Sanh, because he was such a kind, honest, and brave young man.

Princes from neighboring countries, however, did not approve at all. Taking the princess's marriage to a woodcutter as a terrible insult to their honor, they gathered together and invaded the Viet kingdom.

The king summoned all his mandarins to discuss a plan. At the meeting, Thach Sanh volunteered to go to the battlefield. The king offered to give Thach Sanh his royal sword and 20,000 soldiers to accompany him. Thach Sanh refused.

"I'll only need twenty men," he said.

The sight of Thach Sanh and his army of twenty made the neighboring princes roll on the ground with laughter. Thach Sanh ignored them. Without saying a word, he sat down, took out his lute, and played.

The music sounded like wives calling for their husbands, mothers crying for their sons. It reminded the enemy soldiers of their families back in the countryside. It made them unwilling to fight. The music urged them to drop their weapons, to think of peace. A soldier took his armor off and walked away. Two, three, four, then dozens, then hundreds, then thousands of others soldiers joined him. Within minutes, the enemy had lost its desire to fight.

The music made the princes realize how unreasonable they had been. They knelt down and asked Thach Sanh for forgiveness. He insisted that they stand up and be his friends. The princes agreed willingly.

Thach Sanh said, "You've traveled here from very far away. Perhaps you're hungry. We would like to feed you."

The neighboring princes did not believe that Thach Sanh and his twenty men could possibly feed such a huge army of soldiers. When Thach Sanh took out his magic rice pot, one prince said, "Thank you, brother, for thinking of our men. But such a small pot would not provide enough rice for even one of my bodyguards. How could you feed the whole army?"

Thach Sanh smiled. "Let me feed your body-guard first," he said. "If I do not have enough rice, I will apologize for breaking my promise."

One of the guards, obeying his master, stepped forward. He used his fingers, thinking he would finish the rice in one second. But, strangely enough, the more he ate, the fuller the pot became. Finally, when he could eat no more, the pot remained as full as if no one had touched it. Now, the neighboring princes believed that Thach Sanh had magic powers. The former enemies feasted and celebrated together long into the night.

After that, Thach Sanh and the princess lived happily, and the country enjoyed many years of peace.

About the Authors and Illustrator

ᖇᖇᖇᖇᖇᖇᖇᖇᖇᖇᖇᖇᖇᖇᖇᖇᖇᖇᖇᖇᖇᖇᖇᖇ

Nguyen Nguyet Cam is a Vietnamese language instructor at the University of California, Berkeley. She is the co-translator of *Dumb Luck*, a novel by Vu Trong Phung. She has published numerous translations of works from English into Vietnamese, including two of E. B. White's classic children's novels, *Charlotte's Web* and *The Trumpet of the Swan*.

Dana Sachs is the author of *The House on Dream Street: Memoir of an American Woman in Vietnam*. She is the co-translator of Le Minh Khue's collection of short fiction, *The Stars, The Earth, The River*. Her articles, reviews, and essays about Vietnam and Vietnamese culture have been published widely. She lives in North Carolina.

Bui Hoai Mai, a graduate of the Hanoi Fine Arts College, has exhibited his paintings and his photographs in solo shows in Vietnam and Europe. His artwork has been purchased for collections throughout the world. In addition, he studies, collects, and writes about ancient Vietnamese ceramics. He lives in Hanoi and Bac Ninh, Vietnam.

Production Notes for Sachs/TWO CAKES FIT FOR A KING

Cover and interior designed by Trina Stahl in Janson Text,
with display type in Pompeii Capitals

Composition by Trina Stahl

Printing and binding by Versa Press, Inc.

Printed on 60# Starbrite Opaque, 435 ppi

ML   1 / 05